11. Dauphin — p.8

12. dissolute — p.9

13. victuals — p.9

14. underlings — p.9

15. Bastille — p.10

16. treachery — p.10

17. partition — p.10

18. Regent — p.11

19. imbecile — p.11

20. adherents — p.12

21. piety — p.12

22. indolent — p.12

23. languid — p.13

24. asunder — p.13

The Joan of Arc

E. M. Wilmot-Buxton

DOVER PUBLICATIONS, INC.
Mineola, New York

25. stolid *p. 14*

26. usurper *p. 15*

EDITOR OF THIS VOLUME: JENNY BAK

27. escutcheons *p. 15*

28. austere *p. 15*

29. Ave *p. 16*

30. Paternoster *p. 16*

31. pious *p. 16*

32. marauder *p. 17*

Bibliographical Note

This Dover edition, first published in 2004, is a republication of *Jeanne D'Arc,* originally published in 1914 by Frederick A. Stokes Company, New York. The plates have been omitted from this edition.

Library of Congress Cataloging-in-Publication Data

Wilmot-Buxton, E. M. (Ethel Mary)
    [Jeanne d'Arc]
    The story of Joan of Arc / E.M. Wilmot-Buxton.
       p. cm.
    Originally published: Jeanne d'Arc. New York : Frederick A. Stokes Company, 1914.
    ISBN 0-486-43754-X (pbk.)
    1. Joan, of Arc, Saint, 1412–1431. 2. Christian saints—France—Biography. 3. France—History—Charles VII, 1422–1461. I. Title.

DC103.W52 2004
944'.026'092—dc22

                           2004053732

Manufactured in the United States of America
Dover Publications, Inc., 31 East 2nd Street, Mineola, N.Y. 11501

Contents

THE MAID

Thunder of riotous hoofs over the quaking sod;
Clash of reeking squadrons, steel-capped, iron-shod;
The White Maid and the white horse, and the flapping banner of God.

Black hearts riding for money; red hearts riding for fame;
The Maid who rides for France and the King who rides for shame—
Gentlemen, fools, and a saint riding in Christ's high Name!

"Dust to dust!" it is written. Wind-scattered are lance and bow,
Dust, the Cross of St. George; dust the banner of snow.
The bones of the King are crumbled, and rotted the shafts of the foe.

Forgotten, the young knight's valour; forgotten, the captain's skill;
Forgotten, the fear and the hate and the mailed hands raised to kill;
Forgotten, the shields that clashed and the arrows that cried so shrill.

Like a story from some old book, that battle of long ago:
Shadows, the poor French King and the might of his English foe;
Shadows, the charging nobles, and the archers kneeling a-row—
But a flame in my heart and my eyes, the Maid with her banner of snow!

THEODORE ROBERTS
By permission of the Editor of the "Pall Mall Magazine."

I

THE FALL OF FRANCE
1350–1400

La Gloire est morte

IN the great gallery of Versailles stands the white marble figure of a maiden, young and slender in her knightly armour, her peaked face bent pensively earthward, a sword hilt clasped between her strong young hands.

It is Jeanne d'Arc, the Maid of France, a figure startling in its almost childish simplicity, but by which the fifteenth century is dominated as completely as is the thirteenth by St. Francis of Assisi or the early part of the nineteenth by Napoleon Buonaparte.

Yet for how short a time did the vision of the Maid flash forth upon the startled and incredulous eyes of France.

A little more than a year saw her task accomplished, her reputation won and lost, her story told. And when we realize that the task set before her of saving her country from complete domination by a foreign power was carried out to its successful issue by a girl—a mere child, for she was only nineteen years of age when she was called upon to die—it will be hard indeed to deny the fact that in her we see one of the most striking marvels in history.

In vain does a modern compatriot of the Maid[1] try to belittle her, treating her achievements as the result of a mixture of good fortune and sound common sense, and with odd inconsistency her visions as the fancies of a neurotic girl. If that be so, as another critic[2] has remarked,

---

[1] M. Anatole France.
[2] Andrew Lang.

"the marvel becomes a miracle, and the miracle has to be explained away." For the fact remains that this untaught peasant maiden, at an age when most girls of to-day would, according to their position, be just leaving school, or looking out for a place as under-nurserymaid, proved herself the equal of warriors and politicians, led armies largely disaffected to victory, worsted her foes by her superior military tactics, and ultimately saved France from downfall and subjection.

To understand fully the conditions under which this amazing task was accomplished we must try to get a clear idea of the state of the country for which Jeanne the Maid laid down her life. We must take ourselves in imagination back to the latter years of the fourteenth century, long before the little Maid first opened her dark eyes upon her "sweet land of France," in order to understand the urgency of her call and the greatness of her achievement.

The last quarter of the fourteenth century was a time of unrest and revolt throughout the whole of Western Europe. In Italy, in France, in Germany, in England, a spirit of discontent with the ruling powers, of demand for more equal distribution of the goods of this world, of rebellion against the spell of servitude which the Feudal System had cast over the "common folk," as Froissart calls them, was moving upon the face of the whole land. In England it led to the Peasants' Revolt under Wat Tyler; in France to the outbreak known as the Jacquerie; in Germany to the society named in scorn "The Beghards."

Such upheavals are no doubt necessary from time to time, if only to maintain the balance of justice between man and man; but the actual period in which they occur is invariably one of acute misery and suffering for the poor and weak, and their immediate consequences are, as a rule, far from beneficial to any class of society.

The extraordinary event which marked the closing years of Charles V of France had much to do with this condition of unrest and unsettlement. The most stable fact in Europe, for the last thousand years, had been the position of the Pope, the successor of St. Peter, as Head of the Holy Catholic Church throughout Christendom. To Rome turned the eyes of all men; for there, in the Pontiff's chair, sat not only the spiritual Head of the Church, but a great temporal ruler, swaying the minds of kings. Early in the fourteenth century, however, when Pope Clement had fallen a prisoner into the hands of Philip IV of France, this vast power had been shaken to its foundations, and for seventy years the popes were forced to hold their court at the French city of Avignon instead of at Rome, and to bow to the will of the kings of France. This was a terrible blow to the dignity and reputation of the Papacy, but worse was to come.

In 1378 the "Great Schism of the West" divided Europe into two hostile camps; for one Pope ruled in Rome and claimed the allegiance of the Catholic Church, and another at Avignon made the same claim, while acting merely as the puppet of the French king. The unity of the Church seemed threatened; and all Christendom stood aghast at the spectacle of France, Scotland, and the little kingdoms of Castile and Naples supporting the worldly and self-seeking Clement VII at Avignon; while Northern Italy, Germany, England, and most of the Northern States of Europe acknowledged the supremacy of Urban VI as he wielded his stern sceptre from the seat of St. Peter at Rome.

While this strange state of affairs was shaking the foundations of Europe and causing terrible scandal to the Faith, the death of Charles V in 1380 placed the crown of France upon the head of a handsome boy of eleven years old, who was, through little fault of his own, to bring ruin and desolation upon his country. With grim foreboding of this fact, his father had said to the boy's uncles, the Dukes of Berri and Burgundy, and Bourbon, brother to the Queen, "In you I put my whole confidence; the boy is young and fickle-minded, and there is much need that he should be guided and governed by good teaching." But in those days such a thing as loyalty to a boy ruler did not

exist. The one aim of Burgundy was to secure the important domain of Flanders and thus make himself un-
disputed ruler of the whole of Northern and Eastern
France. Berri cared only for the coarse pleasures obtained
with the money he wrung from the peasants of the South;
Bourbon counted for nothing in the scale of right; Anjou,
eldest of the late king's brothers, was a man of vast ambition, whose determination to win for himself the kingdom
of Naples and Sicily kept him out of France during most of
the coming period.

The frequent quarrels of these "Princes of the Lilies,"
the greed with which they grasped at the treasure, plate
and jewels of their late brother, and the eagerness with
which each determined to make himself supreme in one
part or another of France, boded ill for a reign of peace
and unity; and the boy-King, Charles VI, found himself,
from the first, overwhelmed in a maze of intrigues, revolts
and petty wars. When Flanders, under the brave Philip
van Arteveldt, struck a plucky blow for freedom from the
yoke of Burgundy, the young King was induced to march
against him; and the crushing vengeance dealt, after the
fall of Philip, to the most industrious and peaceful of the
subjects of the French crown, marked only too clearly
the survival of the old bad spirit of the feudal lord
towards his inferior.

Almost at the same moment, Paris and other leading
cities of France had seized the chance to revolt against
the ever-growing burden of taxation, but the triumph of
Charles in Flanders put an end to all hope of redress.
Dismay fell upon the citizens as they bowed their necks
under the foot of the conquering nobles, who proceeded
to make their burdens even heavier than before.

These events of the beginning of the reign were typical
of the rest. Yet the character of the young King was not
unattractive. One historian calls him "benign and gentle,"
and says he tried to shelter the conquered citizens from
the horrible vengeance wreaked on them by Burgundy.
But, as his father had said, he was "fickle-minded," fond of

pleasure and self-indulgence, shirking the responsibility of a right judgment and the duties it entailed; and when this volatile lad of sixteen married the fourteen-year-old Isabel of Bavaria, a pretty child who was fated in future years to be the evil genius of the land, the fates that frowned on France in the fourteenth century had almost done their worst.

Yet the people believed in their young King with touching loyalty, putting down to the account of the regent uncles all such mistakes as the dismal failure of an expedition against England in 1386, and an equally dismal attempt upon the Rhine borders of Germany.

They rejoiced therefore when Charles, in his nineteenth year, being at Rheims, the religious capital and the ancient coronation place of the French kings, suddenly threw off the yoke of the Dukes of the Lilies, dismissing them "right well and graciously, with many thanks for the trouble and toil they had had with him and with the realm."

The fact that he proceeded to choose his counsellors from his father's old friends, making Oliver Clisson Constable of France, did not sweeten the bitterness of dismissal to the royal uncles, who went off, Berri to the South, Burgundy to his own province, breathing ill-content and hostility with every breath they drew.

The Duke of Berri, indeed, had soon good cause to show his wrath in the open; for the King, in a brief fit of anxiety to relieve his long-suffering people from the shameful burdens placed upon them by the Duke, deposed his uncle and made him thenceforth his bitter enemy.

Meantime, however, there was coming upon Charles a dark hour destined to exact a penalty for his weakness and self-indulgence that more than avenged the irate Duke of Berri.

A certain Peter Craon, a follower of the Duke of Orleans, brother to the King, had been dismissed from Court by the wish of Clisson, the Constable. In revenge this man awaited Clisson on the highway one dark night, set upon him and left him for dead in the wayside ditch. News of this was carried to the King's bedside by one of the men-at-arms of the unfortunate Constable, and Charles hastened there and then to find his body. Clisson, however, though sorely hurt, was already beginning to recover; he was able to denounce his assassin by name, and upon Craon Charles vowed a deadly vengeance. Craon, however, had fled to the Duke of Brittany, who promptly showed his contempt for the Crown by refusing to give him up. The King's uncles advised him to drop the matter; Clisson and his friends were bent on vengeance; and forthwith the King, feverish and uncertain in health, and against the advice of the physicians, set out with his army against the rebellious Duke in a very hot August.

No doubt he brooded secretly on the wrong done to his friend; no doubt also his self-indulgent life had sown the seeds of mind trouble, for as he rode along under a hot summer sun, he was unreasonably startled by the appearance of a wild-eyed man, some wandering lunatic, who rushed from the woods to seize his bridle and to cry aloud, "Go no further; you are betrayed to your enemies!"

The man was driven off, no one paid much heed to the white face and staring eyes of the King, and the cavalcade moved on again. Suddenly, as the heat grew stronger, a page who rode just behind him dozed and nodded, letting his spear fall with a rattle on the helmet of another who rode close by. At the clatter the King's nerve suddenly gave way. With a shriek of "Treason!" he drew his sword, and before he could be hindered, had slain four of his company. He had quite suddenly become a madman, and though there were times when he returned to something resembling sanity, he was never again entirely responsible for the government of his country.

Thus was the doom of France sealed for the next fifty years; for, in the hands of a wicked Queen, selfish and scheming princes and ambitious adventurers, all sense of unity and cohesion was gradually lost, and the land was left at the mercy of a foreign invader.

With one Pope at Rome and another at Avignon, the bond of religious faith, generally the strongest of all to bind a country together, was fast weakening; and even the well-meant efforts of Charles, in one of his more lucid intervals, to put an end to the schism by forcing the French Pope to abdicate only seemed to make matters worse. For France at once split up into definite parties on that very question. The Duke of Orleans and his followers supported him of Avignon, the Duke of Burgundy held with the King that both popes should abdicate, and a third be elected to fill the papal seat at Rome.

These two great parties, the Orleanists or Armagnacs in the South, and the Burgundians in the North and East, began steadily to increase in the fierceness of their rivalry.

A truce of twenty-eight years had been made with England after the marriage of Richard II with the little French princess, Isabel, and this might have given the country an opportunity of recovering after the long nightmare of the Hundred Years War. But with no strong ruler at the head of affairs, with a Queen to whom her subjects merely represented a means of obtaining money for her scandalous amusements, and who was supported by the "aristocratic" party of Orleans, France had no chance.

For even Burgundy, who had some slight pretensions to be considered the "friend of the people," went to the wall at this time in a wild crusade against the Ottoman Turks, failing after a fashion that for a time completely crushed his party and left all power in the hands of the Court— that is, with the Queen and the Duke of Orleans.

And so the gloomy story progresses. On the one hand we see the poor mad King amusing himself with the cards said to have been invented for his diversion; on the other the grim game played by the rival parties, Burgundian against Armagnac, Berri and Bourbon now against one of these, now against each other. The Queen keeps mad revel at her wicked Court; the faces of the peasants are ground that the money may be forthcoming.

When Philip of Burgundy died, his son, John the Fearless, took up the quarrel, posing, as his father had done, as the Friend of the People, and the ally of England.

For a time he carried all before him, and even the Queen and the Duke of Orleans were compelled to acknowledge him as the head of the governing powers. A kind of truce between the two rivals was patched up, and partly owing to Berri's good offices, they so far became reconciled as to appear publicly at Mass together. But within a week Orleans had been foully murdered by a follower of the Duke of Burgundy; and the strange part of the matter is that this black deed was condoned by the Church and approved by all Paris, and even by the muddled brain of the victim's brother, the poor mad King himself.

The feud was taken up by the young sons of the murdered prince, who henceforth represent not only the aristocratic faction, but what we may call the national party in France. They were bitterly opposed by the Burgundians, representing the citizen element and the English alliance, who still held Paris; so there now commenced what was practically a civil war between the two factions. Sometimes a truce was patched up, and the two dukes appeared before their troops both riding the same horse in token of that fact. More often the conflict was waged to the death; sometimes Burgundy was worsted and fled to his own domain; sometimes the Armagnacs, on whose side we now find that weak-faced lad, the Dauphin, gave way before the onslaught of the Burgundians and their supporters.

Finally, as far as this period is concerned, a treaty signed at Arras drove the latter to the wall; and the wretched young Prince, who was to hand on to his country the fruit of the legacy of vice bequeathed by his mother to himself, made himself ruler of Paris with the aid of the party of Orleans.

Now there succeeded to the throne of England about that time (1413–1414) a certain young King whose keen eyes saw the weakness and the shoddy character of the man who called himself Regent of France. It did not need the insulting present of tennis balls to decide Henry V to revive the claim his great-grandfather had made upon that country. What better moment could he choose than now, when a mad King in name, a dissolute Prince in fact, ruled over a land torn in pieces by internal strife, crushed by taxation, weakened by long years of misgovernment?

In the war that followed every natural advantage lay with the French. As an English chronicle of that day says of the march from Harfleur to Calais, "Bridges and causeways are broken everywhere; the pomp of the French grows and swells. The King (Henry V) has scarce eight days' food; the French destroy farms, wine and victuals. They sought to weary the people out with hunger and thirst."

Yet the result of this weary march was the tremendous victory of Agincourt, in which the Armagnacs had been so confident of success that they had refused with scorn the offer of the Burgundians to help them in the struggle, as well as the well-meant attempt of the burghers of Paris to support their cause.

The victory struck a deadly blow at the party of Orleans; but in the interval of two years that elapsed before Henry V was able to follow up his success, the old feud broke out again with fresh bitterness. John the Fearless was in reality a weak fellow enough, never able to hold an advantage he had won; the Armagnacs held the person of the King and of his son.

About this time the wretched Dauphin, worn out by wickedness, died; and within a few months, his next brother, a friend to Burgundy, also passed away with suspicious suddenness. For those were the days when the gift of a pair of gloves often meant death by poison to the wearer, and when the food and drink of princes had to be tested by underlings before it was safe for them to partake.

These events made Charles, a boy of fourteen, Dauphin of France. He was a devoted Armagnac, and the Duke of Orleans soon found himself at the head of the

Government. Meantime the infamous Queen Isabel was driven out of Paris by her own son, and exiled; and in her exile she was sought out by the Duke of Burgundy, eager to establish a rival claim, and declared by him to be Regent of France. Together they set up a Parliament at Poitiers, declaring that the Parliament of Paris was dissolved, and forthwith sent spies to tamper with the citizens of the latter city and to make traitors to the cause of Orleans.

Within a short time Paris had rebelled against the strict hand of its new ruler; the Armagnacs were massacred in the streets, the poor mad King led out as though he were on the side of the successful Burgundians; while the Dauphin narrowly escaped and fled to Melun from the Bastille, where he had been shut up by his friends for safety.

Still more fiercely raged the feud, while the Burgundians held Paris and the Dauphin with the Armagnac remnant carried on a disheartened kind of civil war against them.

This was the opportunity for Henry of England to descend once more upon the distracted country. The Duke of Burgundy, together with the Dukes of Anjou and Brittany, at once played false to his country by signing a "treaty of neutrality" with him, and looked on, helpless and inactive, while Henry besieged his chief town, Rouen. Rouen fell, and the English King moved on to Paris; and then it began to dawn on the rival factions that France, as an independent kingdom, would soon be lost if nothing effective was done.

Thereupon an attempt was made to patch up a reconciliation between the representatives of the two great parties, and the old Duke of Burgundy was invited by the boy Dauphin to meet him on the Bridge of Montereau and endeavour to come to terms.

The greatest precautions were taken against treachery. A partition was erected, and the leaders were to speak through a hole in the same; but John of Burgundy, impetuous even in his old age, stepped over the barrier and knelt at the feet of the young Prince. Immediately he was cut down by a blow from Duchâtel, one of the chiefs of the Orleanists, and fell dead upon the bridge.

This treacherous and stupid act sealed the fate of France at that time. It made the new Duke Philip the implacable foe of the Armagnacs, and hence the ally of Henry. It turned the Duke of Brittany, who had also met with treachery at their hands, dead against them, while the Queen was more violently opposed than ever both to her son and his supporters. Hence it was not difficult for these powerful foes to convince the country that the rule of the Englishmen, even though it made France but a province of England, was better than government by a weak, cruel and treacherous young Prince of their own race.

So with little difficulty Henry V arranged the Treaty of Troyes in 1420, by which the English King was declared Regent and heir of France after the death of the imbecile King Charles, and was to marry forthwith the Princess Catherine, his daughter.

All Northern France, either by pressure brought by the army within its borders, or because it hoped that then the long strife might end, agreed to this arrangement and gave its allegiance to Henry and the Burgundians. But south of the Loire the national spirit remained alive; and there the Dauphin, supported by the Armagnacs, now the representatives of the National party, and by bands of Scottish "free lances," was acclaimed as the true heir of Charles VI. Even the men of the South, who had suffered in former days under the hands of this very faction, gave in their allegiance for the sake of preserving the nation from foreign rule.

Just before his end in 1422, the victorious Henry approached Orleans, the chief centre of this opposition to his rule, and threatened to besiege it. But death put a stop to this attempt; and the decease of the unhappy Charles of France some few weeks later left the crown in the weak hands of a baby English Prince of nine months old.

"Long live King Henry of France and England!" shouted the men of the North as the body of King Charles was hastily interred in the cathedral of St. Denis.

The echoes of that strange cry reached the banks of the Loire, bearing hopeless dismay to the heart of the spiritless young Dauphin, who, almost against his will, was proclaimed King forthwith in the chapel of Mehun (1422).

A finer character would, at this juncture, have played the man and made a desperate bid for the recovery of the North of France; for the English cause, wholly dependent as it was upon the alliance of Burgundy, was far from strong, in reality, at this time.

But Charles VII was to be no hero-King. The utmost that can be said for him by his warmest adherents is that he was "a handsome prince, well-languaged and full of pity for the poor, with a very sincere piety." He had no initiative, no will to do the right thing at any cost. Indolent by nature, and hating the sight of battlefields, he inherited his father's weak mind, his mother's love of luxury and ease.

In after days, only one voice was raised in defence of a King who was accused of "always wishing to hide from his people in castles and holes and corners"; and that was the voice of the little Maid who was to lay down her life for one to whom she had generously given the devotion of her innocent heart.

At this time, however, Jeanne was a ten-year child, dreaming among the daisied meadows of Domrémy, and France was left to rush blindly on her fate.

The English Duke of Bedford was proclaimed Regent of France, and governed Normandy, Paris and the North with an iron hand. South of the Loire a civil conflict was raging, and devastating the whole country.

In one battle (Beaujé, 1421) the Scottish allies of the Dauphin won a victory and slew the Duke of Clarence, uncle to the English King. Three years later came the almost total extermination of the Scots at Verneuil (1424), a defeat which determined the Dauphin to risk

no more battlefields. From that time he wandered list-
lessly from town to town, where he could still count on
some measure of loyalty, sometimes making empty and
languid efforts towards negotiations with Burgundy at
the pressure of his chief partisan, the Archbishop of
Rheims.

For the Dauphin was but a puppet-prince. Completely in
the hands of the men who had brought about the murder
of the late Duke of Burgundy on that bridge of Montereau,
how could he hope to accomplish a sound alliance with
the murdered man's son? Could he have summoned up
spirit to banish these advisers, de Richemont, Constable
of France, and son of the Duke of Brittany, would have
stood his friend and brought about an alliance that would
have driven the English from France.

But it was left to de Richemont to get rid of these
favourites by murder and treachery, without advancing
any nearer the end in view. He only became an object of
intense hatred to the Dauphin, who had now found a new
favourite in de Trémoille. The leading characteristic of
this man was that he was a "double traitor" both to the
House of Burgundy, in whose employ he had been, and to
de Richemont, who represented the party of the Dauphin;
so that at the very moment that the English were preparing to take Orleans by storm, the forces of the Prince were
under the rival leaderships of the banished de Richemont
and de Trémoille.

This, then, was the problem which had to be dealt with
by the future Saviour of France: a country weakened by
fifty years of faction and civil war, torn asunder by a foreign invader, as well as by internal strife; possessing no
leader of note, no sovereign capable of inspiring a loyal
devotion to his cause; with an army ill-trained, disaffected
and disheartened by recent failure; a country, lastly,
whose central point, the city of Orleans, was so sorely
threatened by the English that it seemed as though the
"key of the South" would shortly fall into the foeman's
hands.

II

THE MAID OF DOMRÉMY

La grande pitié qu'il y avait au royaume de France
(Les Voix)

THE little village of Domrémy lies on the banks of the
Upper Meuse, the river that forms the boundary
between France and the Duchy of Lorraine.

It must have always been a straggling little place, surrounded by hills and oak forests, but itself lying low, with
meadows apt to be swamped by the autumn overflow of
the river, and vineyards sloping gently back to the rising
ground in the distance.

Just across the river, the rival village of Maxey stood
firm for the Burgundians and for the English King; and no
doubt the children of Domrémy often reproduced the
strife that was raging in France, when they went forth
armed with stones and sticks "for the cause of the King"
to strike a blow at the "traitors" of Maxey, the boys and
girls across the water.

Higher up the Meuse stood the walled city of
Vaucouleurs, the capital of the district, held at that time
for the Dauphin by the Seigneur, Robert de Baudricourt,
who was to play no unimportant part in the history of
Jeanne.

Here, then, in this outlying corner of the champagne
district, lived the worthy peasant-farmer, Jacques d'Arc, a
good, steady, unimaginative man, wholehearted in his
care for his little family and for the horses and sheep and
pigs which he owned. It was he who, first among the vil-
lagers, saw the advantage of renting, together with six
others, that curious place known as the "Castle of the
Island" for the protection of families and cattle in case of
attack from Burgundian or English foes.

A deserted feudal castle, surrounded by a wonderful
old garden and a deep moat, was no bad playground for
an imaginative child; and little did stolid Jacques d'Arc

reck of the dreams that were dreamed there by his little daughter Jeanne, while his boys Jacques and Jean and Pierre were off and away with pockets full of stones wherewith to quell the bold spirits of the Maxey lads who stood for the cause of the usurper.

Not that Jeanne was permitted to waste much time in day-dreaming in her Castle of the Island. She had a good, religious, practical mother, Isambeau by name, who, though she saw no need to teach her little daughter to read and write, would have her busy with skilled needle-work, to say nothing of the necessity of spinning flax into linen for shirts for her father and the boys. When in after days she was asked if she had been taught any art or trade, she could answer with innocent pride, "Yes, my mother taught me to sew and spin, and so well indeed that I do not think any lady in Rouen could teach me more."

One who has visited[1] the humble home of the Maid in Domrémy describes the place as a little grey cottage, covered with a wild vine which almost hides the primitive carving over the door. But there can still be distinguished with difficulty the narrow escutcheons containing the royal arms of France, with the device *Vive le Roy Loys;* and the armoral bearings granted by Charles VII to the Maid— a drawn sword of silver, the point of which supports a royal crown.

Within the house is seen the dark and gloomy "chambre de famille," where little Jeanne passed many an hour of her young life in needlework or knitting under the eye of her mother. It is sparsely furnished, and still retains the austere appearance of former days.

Darker and still more austere is the little room beyond, where Jeanne dreamed her girlish dreams and slept the healthy sleep of childhood. Formerly it served also as the family bakehouse, and the place where the oven was built is still visible in the corner of the room.

---

[1]Mlle de Bazelaire—*Figure Exquise.*

The cupboard where Jeanne hung her poor little peasant's dress is now only a hole in the wall; and the room itself has the bareness of a cave, touching in its simplicity.

In these surroundings the child was trained to be helpful to her parents and to her neighbours. In later years, when these early days of her life underwent an examination extraordinarily searching and hostile, we have the witness of one Simon, a labourer, to the fact that as a child he was nursed in illness by the little maid from the cottage of Jacques d'Arc, and others told how, when some poor soul sought a night's lodging, she was content to lie by the hearth and give up her bed to the wayfarer. "She was such," they said, "that, in a way of speaking, all the people of Domrémy were fond of her." She was certainly, from the first, a deeply religious little maiden. From the days when she learnt her *Ave* and her *Paternoster* at her mother's knee, the ruined chapel of the Castle, the little grey village church, drew the child with cords of love.

It was said of her that "she often went to church when others went to dance"; to the church that stood so close by her cottage home, and which, for her, was full of the memories of saints and angels.

The building itself was dedicated to St. Remy, and so she would be familiar with the story that tells how an angel brought the holy oil to the saint, by which henceforth every king of France must be consecrated at his own city of Rheims. Probably from the lips of her mother or from the village *curé,* who must have had a very tender spot for this pious little member of his flock, she heard also the story of St. Margaret and St. Catherine, with whose images she was familiar in the church; and she had also a special devotion to St. Michael the Archangel, a favourite saint in France, for to him belonged that great castle in Normandy of which every child had heard, since it was one of the few that yet held out against the English.

With these and other saints did Jeanne hold converse, and to them she paid her little devotions just as Catholic children have always done; and beyond the fact that she loved more than the rest to hear the bell ring for daily Mass and left the dance gladly to go and pray in church, she was no more devout or mystically inclined than most little Catholic maids of eleven or twelve. Simple homely work, simple homely faith, those were the chief influences that touched the early life of the Maid of France at this time.

Gradually, however, other impressions began to overshadow her young soul. Through the village troops of soldiers on their way to garrison duty at Vaucouleurs during the active season of the war, or preparing to give their forty days' service, must have passed from time to time. Sometimes, too, their fierce neighbours, the Duke of Lorraine and the Damoiseau de Commercy, made plundering raids upon these peaceful villages on the banks of the Meuse. On one of these Jeanne said that "she helped well in driving the beasts from and to the island castle, named the Island, for fear of the men-at-arms."

Then faces, once familiar in Domrémy, began to disappear and be seen again no more. "He is gone to the war." "He was killed in the siege"; such sayings fell not unheeded on the ears of the Maid, as she noted the absence of here a cousin and there a friend. Once at least the cattle of the village were driven off by a marauder, and though they were recovered, such an exciting event for quiet Domrémy would have had a marked effect upon a sensitive, intelligent child, who at that time had already received, as far as we can judge, a strange mysterious message from an unknown source. "What is the war about?" She must have asked the question long ere this; and from whatever quarter the answer came, whether from father or mother, village priest or wandering friar, the effect of the story must have been to have raised an ever-increasing "pity for the fair realm of France" in the simple, innocent heart of little Jeanne.

One other influence of her early days must be noticed, since of it her enemies strove to make such evil use in days to come. Within sight of her doorstep was the gloomy Oak Forest, the home of wolves, said to be haunted by fairies, not always "good folk," but more like the "dark ladye" who brought ill-luck to all her lovers.

Legend, vague and obscure enough, based upon a prophecy of the ancient seer Merlin, said that from the Oak Wood should come a marvellous maid for the healing of the nations; and some years before the birth of Jeanne this had crystallized into a prophecy, more detached and precise, to the effect that "A maid who is to restore France, ruined by a woman, shall come from the marches of Lorraine." The reference to the "woman" is, of course, to the wicked Isabel, wife of Charles VI, and this popular version was common property among the whole neighbourhood.

Now some would have it that in this prophecy we have the whole source of the "suggestion" that inspired the Maid to go forth on her mission; and such folk would see that dark Oak Wood constantly haunted by the presence of the Maid, would even see her influenced by the powers of witchcraft, said to pervade its gloomy shades.

But apart from the fact that on her own assertion Jeanne, though she knew the popular version given above, never heard of the Merlin prophecy of the "Oak Wood" till it was told her *after* she had begun her task, we have plenty of witnesses to the fact that the wood had no fascination for the girl. Perhaps she was too well satisfied with the mystical company of saints and angels, which were the daily intimates of every devout Catholic child, to be interested in the tales of fairies and witches which attracted more worldly minds. She said in later days that she had "heard the talk of these things, but she did not believe in it." But since she was of a singularly gay and happy nature, and very far from being a morbid, introspective damsel, she undoubtedly used to join in the May day revels about one of these great forest oaks, dancing with the merry children round the trunk, and hanging garlands on the boughs. "She never knew there were fairies in the wood," she said; and only a dark and perverted mind would see in this innocent amusement of the child Jeanne anything that could possibly be connected with the powers of darkness.

Rather, her lack of interest goes to prove that Jeanne was a normal, healthy-minded child, sensible and practical, by no means given to credulous fancies; and if she were rather more devout than most children of her age, her prayers and love of the Sacraments were anything but a hindrance to the fulfilment of her daily duties. "She was modest, simple, devout," says one who knew her in those years, "went gladly to church and to sacred places; worked, sewed, hoed in the fields, and did what was needful about the house."

This, then, was the life of the Maid of Domrémy until her thirteenth year, up to which time no shadow of foreboding as to the extraordinary task that lay in front of her seems to have crossed her sunny path.

III

THE CALL
1424–1428

Jeanne, soyez sage et bonne
(First Message of the Angelic Voice to Jeanne)

THE year 1424 opened ill for the land of France. It saw a terrible defeat of the Dauphin's forces at Verneuil, where his brave Scottish allies were slaughtered almost to a man; and, though in the months that followed, the great houses of Lorraine and Anjou threw in their lot with the French rather than with Burgundy, there seemed less chance than ever of Charles VII being crowned king of France.

To little Domrémy, on the far borders of Lorraine came grim rumours of the state of Northern France, where, as we learn, "the open land from the Loire to the Somme was a desert overgrown with wood and thickets; wolves fought over the corpses in the burial grounds of Paris; towns were distracted by parties, villages destroyed; the highways ceased to exist; churches were polluted and sacked; castles burnt; commerce at a stand; tillage unknown."

It might indeed have been said by the despairing peasants of the country-side, as in the days of our own King Stephen, that "God and His Saints were asleep," had it not been for very striking evidence to the contrary, shown in a revelation of that year made, not to the wise men of France, not to the great soldiers or the skilled courtiers, but, as once before in the world's history, to the pure vision of a Maid.

It was about the midday hour on one hot summer morning that Jeanne d'Arc sat in the garden of her father's house, busy at her needlework. The sunny air, full of the song of birds and the humming of bees, had just vibrated to the sound of the Angelus bell rung from the steeple close by; for the garden and the churchyard joined, so that Jeanne sat close under the shadow of the grey walls.

Of what was she dreaming as she plied her busy needle? No doubt the "long, long thoughts" of maidenhood were hers, dim and formless enough, and still entwined, perhaps, in her devout young soul with memories of "her brothers the Saints" to whom she had prayed at Mass that morning. But with them there may have mingled deep emotions of pity for the sad condition of her native land, and vague, timid longings that one might be found, even at this eleventh hour, to come to its aid and to cause the uncrowned Dauphin to fulfil his destiny as crowned king of France. But where was that Helper to come from? And how could others, she herself perhaps, help, if only a little, to mend the great wrong that had come upon the land?

Suddenly there falls upon the shady churchyard a beam of light; and a mysterious Voice speaks to the frightened little Maid. It brings no startling message, no sudden call to arms. It is simplicity itself. "Jeanne, sois sage et bonne enfant; va souvent à l'église." Three times she hears it, and so "she knows it for the voice of an Angel." Let us hear her own childlike account as given to her judges a few years later:

"When I was about thirteen years old I had a Voice from God to help me in my conduct. And the first time I was in great fear. It came, that Voice, about midday, in summer time, in my father's garden."

Hoping to prove it to be a hallucination due to bodily weakness, they asked her if she had fasted on the previous day; to which she replied that she had not. Asked how she knew the Voice was, as she said, "for her soul's health," she replied, "Because it told me to be good, and to go often to church; and *said that I must go to France.*"

How soon the latter part of the call was given we do not know, but as Jeanne said that these Voices spoke to her twice or thrice a week it was probably not long before the two admonitions became one command—the call to prepare herself by a holy life for the salvation of her country.

It was long, however, before the child realized that the call was a real actual summons to action. The thing seemed impossible. That she, an ignorant peasant girl, who had never left her native village, could do anything to help the lost realm was too incredible for words.

"Be good!"—yes, she would make *that* her aim. "Go often to church"—to pray for the unhappy land—she was prepared for *that*. But "go to France"—how could this thing be?

Before long, however, the message became yet more definite. In the words of one to whom she confided the experience in later years, "She, with some other girls who were watching the sheep in the common meadow, ran a foot race for a bunch of flowers or some such prize. She won so easily and ran so fleetly that in the eyes of lookers-on her feet did not seem to touch the ground. When the race was over, and Jeanne, at the limit of the meadow, was, as it were, rapt and distraught, resting and recovering herself, there was near her a youth who said, 'Jeanne, go home, for your mother says she needs you.' Believing it to be her brother or some other boy of the neighbourhood, she went home in a hurry.

"Her mother met and scolded her, asking her why she had come home and left her sheep.

" 'Did you not send for me?' she asked.

" 'No!' replied her mother.

"She was about to return to her playmates, believing that some one had played a trick upon her, and may indeed have reached the secluded spot where the sheep were feeding when 'a bright cloud passed before her eyes and from the cloud came a voice saying that she must change her course of life and do marvellous deeds, for the King of Heaven had chosen her to aid the King of France. She must wear man's dress, take up arms, be a captain in the war, and all would be ordered by her advice.'"

The effect of such a call as this upon a normal, healthy, yet sensitively religious girl of thirteen can be easily imagined. At first blank incredulity, then wondering faith, and lastly, humble acquiescence in the Will of God.

By her own account she told no one of the Visions, neither mother nor father, nor even the priest to whom she made her confession. This is surely no matter for surprise. The shrinking from the inevitable astonishment and ridicule of her elders, indeed, from the inevitable admonitions to take a less exalted view of her lot in life, was natural enough. For Jeanne was a very human little maid; and we know that when, after the first call, she became much more devout, going oftener to church, and deserting the dance and the May Tree, she flushed with shame and annoyance when the village boys teased her for being "unco' good." There must, in fact, have been a long struggle in her young mind before she could bring herself to accept the call, even while she still waited for practical means to fulfil it. For three or four years she heard her Voices and almost resisted their commands. Even in 1428, when they became far more explicit and bade her go to Robert de Baudricourt, who would send her with an armed escort to raise the siege of Orleans, she replied in doubt and distress, "I am but a poor girl, who cannot ride or be a leader in war."

For these first years, indeed, she seems to have been content to listen to her Voices without any thought of an immediate summons to action. Not always did they appear to her in bodily form—it is curious that she persistently speaks of "Mes Voix," not of personal apparitions of the Saints, though these did actually appear at times. Three of them became familiar to her; the first being of noble appearance, with wings and a crown on his head, who told her many things concerning the sad state of France. "She had great doubts at first whether this was St. Michael, but afterwards, when he had instructed her and shown her many things, she firmly believed that it was he." From him the message first came very clearly to the frightened girl. "Jeanne, it is necessary for you to go to the help of the King of France; for it is you who shall give him back his kingdom."

And when the child, trembling before such a terrific task, shed tears of humility and fear, he comforted her, saying, "St. Catherine and St. Margaret will come to your aid."

Then came the visions of these two women saints, whom she "knew because they told her who they were."

"I saw them," she says "with my bodily eyes as clearly as I see you; and when they departed, I used to weep and wish they would take me with them."

Poor little weeping Maid, sad in the thought of the high destiny offered to her, ignorant of the means to fulfil it, yet never refusing, never closing her ears to the call.

Unbearable indeed might the burden have proved, borne as it was in silence and isolation, had it not been for the strong religious spirit of the girl. Like another Maid of other days, the model to all others, she was prepared to say, albeit with shrinking heart:

"Ecce ancilla Domini: fiat mihi secundum verbum tuum."[1]

After these Voices made themselves heard, Jeanne became still more devout and preoccupied with her religion. The village boys laughed at her, but, though she flushed with annoyance, she still left the game and the dance to steal away to the quiet little church where, perhaps, her Voices sounded more clearly than in the garden or on the hill-side. No one seems to have suspected anything, nor, beyond the fact that Jeanne was "religious enough for a nun," dreamt that she was contemplating a step extraordinary indeed for a simple village girl. For, outwardly, she seemed what she was in fact, a strong, healthy, sensible maiden, gay and merry enough, with happy dark grey eyes and a ready smile for every one. Only in solitude were the bright eyes sometimes clouded with doubt and dismay; yet, as the years passed on, they grew ever clearer and more determined as the Voices made more distinct the Call from God.

IV
THE MAID OBEYS
Spring 1428

Adieu, Mengette!
(Last words of Jeanne to her friends at Domrémy)

IT was some time in the spring of 1428 that Jeanne's Voices became more insistent, more explicit.

"Go to Messire de Baudricourt, Captain of Vaucouleurs, and he will take you to the King."

By this time fear had vanished, giving place to quiet confidence; she now awaited only a fitting opportunity. Presently this came in the person of a cousin, or uncle as she called him, by marriage, Durand Lassois, living in

---

[1]"Behold, the handmaid of the Lord; be it unto me according to Thy word."

Little Burey, close to Vaucouleurs, who happened at that time to be paying a brief visit to Domrémy.

"Take me back with you, uncle," we hear the girl saying, hoping thus to obtain some opportunity, perchance, of speech with "Messire de Baudricourt."

This worthy was the great man of the district, a bluff, practical soldier, ready enough with his sword in the frequent petty wars that ravaged the marches of Lorraine, but by no means the kind of man to enter with sympathy into the high aims of a religious enthusiast. The moment was propitious for Jeanne's timid request to her relative. Durand's wife was in a weak state of health and overburdened by household matters, and Jeanne would be of use at such a time. Permission was obtained, and the two set off together on what was to be, for Durand at least, an epoch-making pilgrimage. It was not strange that this kindly rustic should have been Jeanne's first confidant, rather than father or mother. Those who know us best are not always the easiest people to whom to confide our highest aspirations, our tenderest hopes. But this good fellow had always had a good word for "petite Jeanne" of Domrémy, and to him was the first revelation made.

Imagine his astonishment, therefore, when the girl at his side, swinging along with her boyish stride, announced that "she must go to France to the Dauphin, to make him be crowned king."

Probably he stammered out some words of surprise, incredulity, even rebuke; for she next asked him calmly, "Did you never hear that France should be made desolate by a woman and restored by a maid?"

The saying was well known to all the country-side, and Durand had nothing to say in reply. From that time he was a firm, if unwilling, ally of Jeanne.

At her urgent request he went up to the Château of Vaucouleurs and interviewed the Seigneur; it was quite clear to his rustic intelligence that de Baudricourt, apart from the fact that he had been actually named by the angel, was the one to take the first decisive step in such a matter.

So he made his way to the hall where the bluff soldier sat polishing his good sword, and in hesitating speech made his request that he should send a peasant maid from Domrémy to the Dauphin, for the purpose of crowning him king.

We can imagine the rude stare, the loud laugh, and the impatient reply of the Seigneur.

"Box the girl's ears and send her home to her mother!"

So Durand returned, crestfallen, to the waiting Jeanne.

"It is no good; he will do nothing for you!"

But Jeanne was not to be daunted by jeering Seigneurs or half-hearted uncles. From this time the consciousness of supernatural help seems to have been so strong that she no longer faltered, or even thought herself unfit. Her marvellous faith, indeed, is not one of the least wonderful traits of her career. "Take me to him; I must see him myself," she said, and so on Ascension Day, May 13th of the year 1428, the Maid made her first public appearance before the crowd of knights, archers and men-at-arms, who had gathered in the hall of the castle of Robert de Baudricourt, half in curiosity, half in scorn, to see this hare-brained girl.

In her shabby red frock, with a white coif over her short black hair, the Maid entered with that air of simplicity and grave courtesy that always marked her behaviour. One amongst that crowd thus described, in after years, that strange interview:

"She said that she came to Robert on the part of her Lord; that he should send to the Dauphin and tell him to hold out and have no fear, for the Lord would send him succour before the middle of the Lent of next year. She also said that France did not belong to the Dauphin, but to her Lord; but her Lord willed that the Dauphin should be its king, and hold it in command, and that, in spite of his enemies, she herself would conduct him to be consecrated.

"Robert then asked, 'Who was this Lord of hers?'

"She answered, 'He is the King of Heaven.'

"This being done, she returned to her father's house with her uncle, Durand Lassois of Burey."

The effect of this interview upon Robert de Baudricourt is left to our imagination. Astounded he must have been, incredulous probably; but there was something in the quiet assurance of the Maid that may have touched some secret spring in his heart. The least religious of men are often the most superstitious, and the evident impression made upon the young knight, de Poulengy, whose words are quoted above, may have been shared by him. Outwardly, however, he remained a scoffer; and Jeanne, rebuffed but by no means disheartened, returned to her father's house.

The next few months must have been some of the most difficult in the life of the Maid. It was impossible that the good folk of Domrémy should be kept any longer in ignorance of what she believed to be her destiny. Durand Lassois would talk of the interview at Vaucouleurs; communication between Burey and Domrémy would not be infrequent, and we may be sure that the former place had been stirred to gossip and comment on what had passed. The parents of the Maid were overwhelmed with horror at the thought of the presumption of their quiet little daughter, and of the possible fate in store for her.

The good Isambeau would probably show her disapproval only by grave looks and unusual silence; but the heart of Jacques d'Arc, the father, grim French peasant that he was, was full of wrath and gloomy foreboding. He had a dream in which he saw the girl surrounded by armed men, in the midst of a company of rough troopers. Horrified at the idea of his gentle, innocent child in such company, he woke, and telling the dream to his wife and sons in the morning, said impressively, "If I could think that the thing could happen that I dreamed, I would wish that Jeanne should be drowned; and if you would not do it, I should do it with my own hands."

Nothing is harder to bear than a daily atmosphere of suspicion, anger, dark looks and darker words from those we love. In days when a parent possessed unlimited power over his children even to the point of life and death, Jeanne was not even free from dread of corporal punishment of the most severe kind.

"Whip her well and send her home to her father," had been de Baudricourt's reiterated advice to Durand Lassois, and knowing the hard nature of her parent, the girl dared not speak openly of her intentions at home. Sometimes, however, the need of speech became too urgent; and it was on one of these occasions that the Maid observed one day to Michael Lebuin, a boy of about her own age:

"There is a girl between Coussey and Vaucouleurs who in less than a year from now will cause the Dauphin to be anointed king of France."

Half in fun, half in awe, the lad repeated the words to others. No woman is a prophet in her own country, and as Jeanne passed by, her bright young face somewhat overcast by the displeasure at home and the want of sympathy abroad, the gossips pointed at her mockingly, saying, "There goes she who is to restore France and the royal house."

Then evil whispers concerning witchcraft and possession began to be put about the village. "Jeannette has met her fate beneath the Fairies' Tree," said an ill-natured dame; and a brother of the Maid repeated it to her with a jeer.

This roused up the good Isambeau d'Arc to take definite action. She would not have her little Jeanne branded as a witch, or worse, on account of some brain-sick fancies which the silly child had picked up Heaven knows where. The best cure for her was a sensible homely marriage, the cares and troubles of which would soon clear her brain and give her something better to think of.

There seems to have been some lad of the village who, at the instigation of her parents, was willing to declare, nay, even to swear before the ecclesiastical court at Toul that Jeanne had promised to marry him.

But here the Maid stood firm. Neither threats nor persuasion from her parents, nor protestations of affection from her would-be lover had the smallest effect upon her. Her destiny was to save France, not to marry; and obedient child as she had always been, she now became an open rebel. It was no small thing to risk offending a father whose temper was not improved by other worries just at that time. For, at the instigation of Bedford, Regent of France, the Governor of the neighbouring district of Champagne was attempting to bring Vaucouleurs into subjection to the English, and devastating meantime all the villages through which he had to pass. Domrémy was one of these, and knowing what it meant, Jacques d'Arc was forced to take his family and flocks for safety to the market town of Neufchâteau, five miles away.

Once installed there, Jeanne had hopes that peace might come to her through the need of constant watching over the cattle, and that past troubles would be swamped in the present danger and discomfort. To her dismay, she found that her persistent lover, no doubt at the suggestion of her parents, had sworn before the judge at Toul that Jeanne was affianced to him, and asked that measures might be taken to force her to the marriage. Her parents threw all the weight of their opinion against the girl, but here Jeanne's spirit rose to the occasion. "She had made no such promise. She would go to Toul herself and swear it before the judge."

"That is impossible," they told her, painting in vivid terms the long journey on foot involved, by roads infested with men-at-arms, through a devastated country. But Jeanne stood firm. "She had always obeyed her parents in everything save in the matter of the trial at Toul," she said sadly in later days. It was a foretaste of martyrdom, for to some sensitive natures defiance of the wishes of those loved most tenderly is worse than bodily death.

So to Toul she went, encouraged only by her Voices,

which bade her fear nothing; and having won her case went back to face the grim displeasure on her father's countenance.

Back to Domrémy, a wrecked and ruined village, they returned, for Vaucouleurs had fallen, though it had not yet been handed over to the English. Even the church, Jeanne's favourite refuge, had been almost destroyed; and no longer could she creep there for daily Mass and Compline, as to an ark of refuge.

Sadly the autumn must have passed away, nor would its gloom be lightened by news received from the outside world. For the city of Orleans, the key to Southern France, was now beleaguered by the English, who had seized all the smaller towns above and below it on the river, and were building towers around the city itself. If Orleans fell, there was nothing to keep the foe from penetrating into the heart of the kingdom and making themselves masters of the whole land. The knell of French independence had struck, and simultaneously the Voices of the Maid spoke with no uncertain sound. "She must leave her village and go into France."

Not long after the Christmas of that year (1428), her chance came. The wife of Durand Lassois needed help with her young babe, and Jeanne lost no time in urging her uncle to beg her father to let her go to his house. Perhaps Jacques d'Arc hoped thus to change the current of her thoughts, perhaps he feared to offend a relative, though it is strange that he should have allowed the girl to go to one who had already aided and abetted her in what he conceived to be foolish, if not criminal, conduct, With a strong foreboding that she had looked for the last time on the home of her childhood, the Maid went forth. "Good-bye, I am going to Vaucouleurs!" she cried to the children who had been her playmates as they ran to the garden gate to see her pass.

"Good-bye, Mengette," to another girl companion, "God bless thee!" But to the little Hauviette, her bosom friend, she said nothing of her departure; she could not trust herself to say farewell to her. "Whereat," we read, "when she heard of her departure, she (Hauviette) wept bitterly because she loved her so much for her goodness, and because she was her dearest friend."

And so Jeanne d'Arc passed away from Domrémy for ever.

V

THE JOURNEY BEGUN
February 1429

Advienne que pourra
(The last words of de Baudricourt to Jeanne)

AT Petit Burey, where Jeanne was living in the beginning of the year 1429, there was relief from the strain of home disapproval, but not less anxiety as to how her mission was to be fulfilled. The Voices of the Maid had fixed Mid-Lent as the time when she must "be with the King." This was fast approaching, but Jeanne, sewing and spinning in the house of her uncle, and later at that of other friends at Vaucouleurs, was seemingly no nearer accomplishing her purpose than before.

In later years witnesses from the little town spoke in touching words of their memories of the Maid at this time; of her quiet patience, her frequent confessions, her earnest prayers in the Chapel of Our Lady, in the Castle, before the battered image that can still be seen there. But at first all seemed hopeless enough. More than once she managed to gain an interview with de Baudricourt at the Castle of Vaucouleurs, but still he scoffed, though with less assurance, and she was forced to return, downcast but not disheartened, to her hostess. To her she spoke openly and with absolute confidence.

"I must be with the Dauphin by Mid-Lent though I should travel on my knees. I must certainly go, for it is the Will of my Lord. It is by the King of Heaven that this work is entrusted to me. Have you never heard how it has been prophesied that France shall be lost by a woman, and restored by a maid from the Marches of Lorraine?"

These words made a good deal of sensation in the town. Some scoffed, others looked with fresh interest at the tall, bright-faced girl with the earnest eyes, who, in her shabby red dress, had become a familiar figure about their streets.

In the second week of February, one of the scoffers, a careless young man of twenty-seven named Jean de Metz, who knew something of her and her people at Domrémy, met her in Vaucouleurs and said teasingly:

"*Ma mie,* what are you doing here? Must the King be turned out of his kingdom and are we all to be made into Englishmen?"

To which she answered with sweet dignity, "I am here because this is a royal town, and I would ask Robert de Baudricourt to lead me to the King. But Baudricourt cares nothing for me nor for what I say; none the less I must be with the King by Mid-Lent if I wear my legs down to the knees by walking there. No man in the world can recover the kingdom of France, nor hath our King any hope of suc- cour but from myself—though I would far rather be sewing by the side of my poor mother, for this deed suits me very ill. Yet go I must, and the deed I must do, for my Lord wills it."

"And who is your Lord?" asked the youth, half con- vinced, and striving with difficulty to keep up his jesting tone.

"My Lord is God," said the Maid very simply.

The young soldier's defences utterly gave way. Seizing her hands he cried, "Then I, Jean de Metz, swear to you, Maid Jeanne, that God helping me, I will lead you to the King, and I only ask when you are prepared to go."

"Better to-day than to-morrow," she answered with her ready smile. "Better to-morrow than later."

But though Jean meant what he said, he did not want to take the whole responsibility. A chance of shifting it on to other shoulders seemed just at that moment to present itself, for the Duke of Lorraine, having heard the reports of a wonderful Maid who was said to foretell the future, sent for her to Nancy, some sixty miles away. With her on horseback Jean travelled for part of the way, Durand Lassois being her guide and guardian; and since anything was better than inaction, Jeanne's heart beat high with hope. But she found at Nancy only a diseased old man, full of anxiety about his own health, who cared for her concerns only so far as he hoped she could prophesy good things as to his recovery. Boldly the Maid told him she knew nothing of such matters, and begged him to send his son-in-law with an army to lead her into France, where she "promised to pray for his better health." But he, disappointed on finding her only a sensible, clear-eyed maiden instead of the visionary he had hoped, sent her off with four francs for her trouble, and possibly a horse; and so Jeanne was obliged to return once more to Vaucouleurs.

Perhaps it was on this return journey that her Voices again spoke to her, revealing events that as yet had not penetrated so far to the south-east. For immediately she reached the town she seems to have sought out Baudricourt once more and to have said in solemn warning, "In God's name, you are too slow in sending me; for this day, near Orleans, a great disaster has befallen the gentle Dauphin, and worse fortune he will have unless you send me to him."

Still bluff de Baudricourt, though inwardly uneasy, shook his thick head, with a clumsy jest; but some few days later a story in confirmation of Jeanne's words arrived by means of a king's messenger. At Rouvray, in the Battle of the Herrings, on February 12, 1429, the Constable of Scotland, in alliance with the French, had been badly defeated by the English, and a heavy blow had been struck at the Dauphin's cause. "There *must* be something in this girl," Baudricourt seems to have argued when he heard this news; and then a light dawned upon him. She must be bewitched; it is the evil spirit within her that speaks, not herself. Anyway, the matter shall be put to the test.

So, into the kitchen of the good-wife, with whom Jeanne was staying, loomed the sudden apparition of the bluff knight and the priest of the Castle chapel. The woman and the girl, busy with their spinning, sprang up in astonishment; the former was asked to withdraw, and Jeanne, seeing the priest putting on his stole, fell on her knees.

Over her the good man proceeded to utter the words by which evil spirits were exorcised, "If thou be evil, away with thee; if thou be good, draw nigh."

Then the girl understood, and with her gentle, half-reproachful smile, came toward him on her knees.

That settled the matter. Jeanne, in talking of the matter with her hostess, said quietly that the priest had had no right to do this, for he had heard her confession and knew her for what she really was; but the effect upon de Baudricourt was remarkable. From this time, though never an enthusiast in her cause, he no longer treated her as a silly child, but as one to be reckoned with, as a person of consideration. All opposition to her setting off to the Dauphin was dropped, though, either from meanness or from dread of being mistaken in her, he took little share in her equipment. The people of Vaucouleurs, now full of faith in the Maid and of enthusiasm for her mission, subscribed toward her expenses, the main burden of which were borne by Jean de Metz, still her firm friend, and Bertrand de Poulengy, the young officer who had been so deeply impressed by the girl on her first visit to the Castle. The presence of the King's messenger gave added point to her departure, as he was prepared to accompany the little band to Chinon.

One detail of her equipment may have been Jeanne's idea for her own safety, or it may have been first suggested by de Metz, in his fear of the ridicule that might fall upon him were he seen by his gay friends as the cavalier of the peasant maid in her shabby red frock. Jean certainly seems to have asked her if she would consent to ride in boy's dress, to which she readily agreed. Probably her own knowledge of the difficulties of the journey, and of her own ignorance of the art of riding, had already suggested the plan to her.

She rode forth from the "Gate of France," therefore, clad in the dark cloth tunic reaching to her knees, high boots and leggings, and black cap of a page. She was escorted by Colet de Vienne, the King's messenger, Richard the Archer, his squire, and the two young knights, de Metz and de Poulengy, with their two men-at-arms; and all the inhabitants of the little town flocked out to see her depart.

"Go, and let come what will!" growled de Baudricourt, as he handed her a sword, gazing still with puzzled disfavor at the slight boyish figure on the big white horse.

"Turn back, little Jeanne," cried the voice of a woman in the crowd, her heart filled with mother love and pity for the young maid, "you cannot go—all the ways are beset by rough men-at-arms."

But the girl replied with joyful dignity:

"The way is made clear before me. I have my Lord to make the way smooth to the gentle Dauphin; for to do this deed I was born."

And thus the little band rode forth into the night.

VI

AT POITIERS
Spring 1429

Ils étaient grandement ébahis comme une si simple bergère jeune fille pouvait ainsi répondre
(Examination of Jeanne d'Arc)

THAT must have been a strange journey, that eleven days' ride from Vaucouleurs to Chinon, on the Loire.

The heart of the Maid was light and gay, for the first step in fulfilment of her mission had at last been taken.

She had, moreover, in reply to tender messages sent to Domrémy, received a letter of forgiveness from her parents, together with a ring of broad plated gold, inscribed with the names *Jesus, Maria.*

Straight-backed, healthy, long of limb, she sat her great horse, tossing back her short dark hair from her brow, and gazing with bright grey eyes into the dark ways in front of her, as though she already saw the end of her journey ere it had well begun.

Her companions bore a different spirit within their breasts. They had taken a vow before de Baudricourt to protect and honour the Maid, but, beside the fact that they had a long and dangerous road in front of them, they carried chilly doubts at their hearts.

"Will you really do what you say?" Jean de Metz inquired of her, being full of fear of the ridicule that would assuredly cover him should Jeanne prove an impostor.

"Have no fear," she replied, "for my Brothers of Paradise have always told me what I should do, and it is now four years or five since they and my Lord have told me that I must go to the war that France may be recovered."

The men-at-arms, also, possibly, their master, the King's messenger, had even less faith in her. They felt their task an indignity. Who was this village girl that she should require such an escort?

Once, in rude jest, they tried to frighten her by pretending they were set upon by English or Burgundian troops. But the Maid, though she believed them, was not afraid.

"Do not flee! I tell you, in God's name, they will not harm you!" she cried, and her simple courage must have touched even those rough hearts to shame.

Riding by night, and sleeping by day among the straw of some inn-stable by the roadside, the girl bore well the hardships of the journey, her one regret being that it was not considered safe in that hostile country to let her hear Mass every day. Choosing by-ways and avoiding high roads and bridges, the journey was toilsome enough, and four flooded rivers had to be forded ere they could draw a long breath of relief at Gien, in the country of the Dauphin. At Fierbois, a stage nearer to Chinon, she was delighted to find a chapel dedicated to one of her favourite saints, St. Catherine, the patroness of captive soldiers and imprisoned peasants.

In that chapel she said her prayer of faith, and from that place she dictated a letter to the Dauphin, telling him that she had ridden one hundred and fifty leagues to tell him things that would be useful to him, and which she alone knew. She ended with a declaration of loyal affection, in which she may have said that she would recognize him, her "gentle prince," among all others, though in later days she seems to have forgotten this saying, if, indeed, she ever said it.

At midday she set out for the town of Chinon, which had been for some time the refuge of the Dauphin.

> Chinon
> Petit ville
> Grande renom.

So ran the old jingle, dating from the days when the Plantagenet princes lived in the fortress of Coudray, which frowned over the gabled houses of the town. "The great walls, interrupted and strengthened by huge towers, stretch along a low ridge of rocky hill, with the swift and clear river—the Vienne—flowing at its foot," says one of Jeanne's chroniclers; and within these strong walls, the dull-witted, timid young Dauphin strove to forget the miseries of the land, fast slipping from his grasp, in amusements, dancing and games.

The ruling spirit of the Court of Chinon was La Trémouille, that stout, coarse-featured noble "always defeated, always furious, bitter, ferocious, whose awkwardness and violence created an impression of rude frankness."[1]

---

[1]A. France.

The influence of this violent character was the worst thing possible for the faint-hearted Charles. The prince owed La Trémouille money, in security for which he had been obliged to hand over to him many broad lands and fair castles. Without his leave he dared not act even if he would; and it was to La Trémouille's interest, traitor as he was at heart, to make him play the waiting game.

To such a man the coming of the innocent Maid, with her boy's clothes and her pure eyes full of faith and confidence, was a thing to be scoffed at, if it were noticed at all. Probably that little letter of Jeanne to the Dauphin had passed through his rough hands, and been torn up and scattered to the winds as a bit of sheer nonsense; for the Dauphin knew nothing of it when she appeared at the Castle gates, craving leave to see the prince.

"Who was she, and why had she come?" they asked her; to which she simply replied that she had come to relieve Orleans and to cause the King to be crowned at Rheims.

There was a delay of two days while the Court considered her request, and Jeanne was fain to possess her eager soul in patience. Slowly the hours must have passed, as the Maid, weak with her Lenten fast, looked forth from the steep street where she had found lodging to the great grey walls that enclosed one who was ever to her a hero prince, her "gentle Dauphin." Then creeping into the dusky shadows of St. Maurice, the nearest church, Jeanne knelt and prayed, and heard, perchance, repeated there the message now grown familiar to her listening ears:

"Daughter of God, thou shalt lead the Dauphin to Rheims that he may there receive worthily his anointing."

Poor little lonely figure, kneeling there in the cold spring twilight, waiting with such eager longing to fulfil the commands of God! Let us hope that the "good woman" with whom she lodged those two days looked with kindly eyes upon the slim girlish figure and gave her a motherly kiss ere she sought her couch. This is her own simple account of the matter:—

"I was constantly at prayers in order that God should send the King a sign. I was lodging with a good woman when that sign was given him, and then I was summoned to the King."

Whether this "sign" was anything more than a decision on the part of his Council of courtiers that it would be to their interest, possibly to their amusement, to see the strange maiden from Domrémy, we cannot say. Possibly, indeed, Jeanne is referring to that other "sign" given by her to the Dauphin during their first interview, of which so much was made at her trial, and concerning which she was so careful to baffle her questioners rather than betray the "secret of the King."

It was evening when the Maid climbed the steep ascent and passed through the Old Gate that led into the Castle of Chinon. Its vast hall was crowded with armed barons, courtiers in long furred robes, knights and younger nobles in their pointed shoes, tight hosen, and brightly coloured tunics. The brilliant scene was lit up by flaming torches held by pages standing against the walls, which for a moment dazzled the sight of Jeanne as she stood within the great doorway. All eyes were turned upon her, and most of those faces were either openly hostile, contemptuous, or showed a sneering smile of amusement at the sight of the slim young Maid in her boy's dress, her short dark hair flung back from her broad and open brow.

In order to raise a silly laugh at her, the Dauphin, dressed in ordinary clothes, had slipped behind the courtiers into another room, and as she looked about her, with that straight and fearless gaze of hers, there were not wanting those who would try to impose upon her with trickery. "See, there is the Dauphin!" said one, pointing to Charles de Bourbon in his princely robes. Some, with ill-bred chuckles, drew her attention to other gaily dressed nobles. But the Maid did not heed them. Looking quietly from one to another, she waited till Charles entered the hall, and at once, going up to him, knelt before him saying:

"God send you life, gentle Dauphin."

The prince, somewhat out of countenance at the failure of his practical joke, peevishly asked her name.

"I am Jeanne the Maid," she answered.

"And what do you want of me, Jeanne?"

"The King of Heaven sends me to succour you and your kingdom, and to conduct you to Rheims to be crowned."

The absolute simplicity and perfect confidence of the words seem to have gone straight to the heart of Charles, who drew her aside and held her in earnest conversation.

At what passed on that occasion we can but guess. Much has been made of some "secret sign" given by Jeanne by which the Prince openly declared he had been most deeply impressed. But what this was the Maid herself would never reveal; and we can but conjecture, from the hints dropped in after years by one of the few confidants of the King, that Jeanne had revealed her knowledge of his secret fears and scruples and prayers as to whether he were the true heir to the throne, and had reassured him that all was well with him, and that God intended him to be crowned.

Yet it was impossible for a slow, timid nature, such as that of Charles, to act at once, and the girl was dismissed, though with a due amount of honour. She was lodged in a tower of the Castle, under the care of a good and pious woman, and given a noble young page, Louis de Coutes, to wait upon her.

Now and again she was sent for to hold converse with the Prince and his advisers, but nothing seemed to come of such meetings, and the Maid was fain to pray afresh and weep with annoyance at such delay.

"You hold so many and such long councils," she said to the Dauphin on one occasion, "and I have but a year and a little more in which to finish all my work."

From the first that piteous prophecy was the burden of all her warnings. Why were they so slow to accept Jeanne with confidence? The history of the time provides us with an answer.

At this period, as we have seen, the religious and political state of Europe was in a ferment. The Turks were threatening to overrun Western as well as Eastern Europe; three popes claimed to be Head of Christendom; and no man knew to whom to look with confidence for religious or political truth and righteousness.

Such times have often produced a crowd of impostors pretending to be the saviours of their country. Sometimes they were fanatics, self-deceived; sometimes they were deliberate frauds. Only a few years earlier a woman named Marie of Avignon had talked of a vision in which she had been bidden to arm herself and go fight for the King; and when she shrank from the task, was told that the weapons were not for her but for another Maid, who should shortly arise and liberate France. This event, while it certainly predisposed the ordinary citizens of Chinon to look with awe and favour upon Jeanne, only did harm to her cause with irreligious nobles like La Trémouille or with worldly ecclesiastics who would keep all supernatural matters within their own province; for the success of the Maid would be a reproach, they thought, to them for their failure.

One consolation came to Jeanne in those dark days of waiting. The young Duc d'Alençon, of the blood royal, who had been taken captive at Verneuil, had just returned to Chinon from five years' sojourn in prison, disheartened and weary of the unhappy cause for which he had already suffered. He had been shooting quails in the marshes of the river meadows, when he heard that Jeanne had arrived, and was at that moment talking to the Dauphin. As he entered the hall, his handsome, boyish figure at once attracted the attention of the Maid.

"Who is that?" she asked the Dauphin, and when she heard his name, "Sire, you are welcome," she said, "the more we have of the blood royal here the better."

After the royal Mass next day the Dauphin called the Maid and the young Duke together, with La Trémouille, into his private room to breakfast with him; and there, in company strange enough to a peasant girl, did Jeanne speak boldly to the vacillating Charles, bidding him amend his life and live after the Will of God, bidding him also to place his realm in the hands of the Almighty and in sure confidence to receive it again from Him.

We can see La Trémouille's coarse lips writhe in a scornful smile at the simple earnest words, and the uneasy impatience of the Dauphin. But d'Alençon's nobler nature was struck, as that of Jean de Metz had been, by her sincerity and quiet force. From that moment he was her staunch friend; and almost immediately after their meeting, when they rode out together for exercise in the meadows, Jeanne so won his heart in another way by her pluck and skill in throwing a lance that he made her a present of a horse.

A few days later he took her to the Abbey of St. Florent, where his mother and his young wife were staying. They too were won by the simple good breeding of the Maid, though the poor little wife said pathetically, before they parted, "Jeannette, I am full of fear for my husband. He has just come out of prison, and we have had to give so much money for his ransom that gladly would I entreat him to stay at home." To which the Maid replied, "Madame, fear not, I will bring him back to you in safety, either as he is now, or better."

We cannot wonder that the girl preferred the character of her "beau Duc," now full of energy for the fight as well as of confidence in her as a leader, to the uncertain, weak young King, who would not make up his mind to do anything at all.

At last there was a new stir at the Castle. Something was to be done, some journey undertaken. The Maid was delighted and made her small preparations in eager haste, hoping that she was to be allowed to go straight to Orleans.

Only when she was in the saddle and had ridden some miles did she learn that she was to go to Poitiers, to be examined as to her mission by the university and the local parliament of that town. To her this seemed a heart-

sickening delay; but there is perhaps some excuse for it
when we remember the very critical state of affairs, and
the inevitable line taken by the King's counsellors. To
trust the affairs of the realm, now already tottering to its
fall, to a peasant girl utterly unversed in matters of warfare, where great soldiers like Dunois and statesmen like
La Trémouille had failed, seemed nothing less than ludicrous. "But what if she be sent by God? Is it not possible
that the Divine help may overcome her natural difficulties?" the Dauphin might have argued. And the Church of
that day would reply with cold and superior scorn, "How
are we to know that she is divinely sent? How does she
differ from Marie d'Avignon and many another visionary
and impostor? What is to be the proof?"

We cannot think it strange that they hesitated; the
stranger thing is that, when Jeanne came before this hostile array, she certainly did, to a great extent, manage to
convince it.

Loathing the delay as she did, the whole thing must
have been a cause of deep irritation and annoyance to the
girl; and though she had always been humble and rever-
ent toward the authority of the Church, she almost lost
her temper with some of her questioners—Dominican
monks, who strove to bully her and who were answered
with the rough directness of an angry girl.

"You say," said one of these, "that God will deliver
France; if He has so determined He has no need of men-at-
arms."

"Oh! can't you see?" she cried, impatiently. "In God's
name the men-at-arms will fight, and God will give the
victory."

"What language does the Voice speak?" said one who
himself talked in broad dialect.

"A better language than yours!" she answered sharply,
perhaps detecting the scornful inflection of his words.

The questioner seems to have lost his own temper at
this thrust, for he asks her abruptly:

"Do you believe in God?"

"More firmly than *you* do!"

"Well, God does not wish us to believe in *you* without better evidence. We cannot advise the King to entrust you with men-at-arms on your word alone, and risk their lives, unless you can show us a sign."

"In God's name!" cried the Maid, "I did not come to Poitiers to give signs! Take me to Orleans, and I will show you the signs of my sending; give me few men or many, but let me go!"

Still, however, the wearisome examination dragged on. Interview followed interview, till the girl was heartily sick of the whole thing. Rashly, perhaps, she confided to her friend d'Alençon, that "she had been much questioned, but she knew and could do more than she had confided to the inquirers"; and this may have accounted for their uncertainty. They felt the power in reserve, and were unwilling to acknowledge it, but they had to do so in the end.

"The Maid's character has been studied; inquiry has been made into her past life, her birth, her intentions; for six weeks she has been examined by clerks, churchmen, men of the sword, matrons and widows. Nothing has been found in her but honesty, simplicity, humility, maiden-hood and devotion. . . . She may go therefore with the army, under honourable superintendence."

Thus was won the first victory over sloth, and doubt, and suspicion. Every effort had been made to rake up something discreditable in her past or present life. To prove her a bold girl, lacking in habits of modesty and dis-cretion, would have settled the question against her. Hence that other examination, hinted here, of discreet widows and matrons, whose sharp eyes and instincts were not likely to be at fault; and the hearts of these good ladies were promptly won by the modesty and purity of the Maid, as those of many of the soldiers and young nobles had been by her pluck and spirit. For let us always see her, not as a pious visionary, full of ecstatic experi-ences that place her above this common earth, but rather, as one of her most sympathetic biographers says, as a clean, honest, public schoolboy, "full of chivalry as of sanctity," fearless in the face of danger, and all the while keeping clear and undimmed the window of her soul.

VII
AT ORLEANS
April 1429

En avant, fille de Dieu, et nous vous aiderons
(Les Voix)

SO at length an expedition was appointed to set out from Chinon to Orleans. It was no mere question of bad roads and fordless rivers that had given the Dauphin pause. He knew but too well that at least three of the strongly fortified towns on the route were in the hands of the English, who also held the banks of the Loire. Faith in the divine mission of the Maid must certainly have increased by this time, for we hear that, when it was proposed to clear the way by driving the foemen from their fortresses, Jeanne was put at the head of the expedition, and orders were given that nothing should be done without her sanction.

So first she goes with a light heart to the city of Tours, a rich and loyal town, held by the mother-in-law of the Dauphin, where her equipment for battle was to be prepared. There, while the suit of "white armour" was being forged by cunning smiths, she procured for herself the sword about which there was so much talk in after days. As she passed through Fierbois on the way to Chinon she had prayed in the Church of St. Catherine, her patron, and had noted there behind, or in front of the altar the tomb of a knight. There need have been no supernatural intervention here; that a knight's tomb should contain his sword was a well-known fact. On the other hand, the devout Maid would prefer that her sword should come to her straight, as it were, from the hands of her own special saint. So she could say with truth to her judges, when they tried to prove witchery in the matter:

"While I was at Tours I sent to seek for a sword in the Church of St. Catherine of Fierbois behind the altar; and presently it was found all rusty. It had five crosses on it, and I knew of it through my Voices. I had never seen the man who went to look for it. I wrote to the Churchmen at Fierbois and asked them to let me have it and they sent it. It was not deep in the earth; I am not certain whether it was behind the altar or in front. When it was found the clergy rubbed it, and the rust readily fell off. The man who brought it was a merchant of Tours who sold armour. The clergy of Fierbois gave me a sheath; the people of Tours gave me two, one of red velvet, one of cloth of gold; but I had a strong leather sheath made for it."

Not only the position of her sword was communicated to Jeanne at this time by her mysterious Voices; she told the Dauphin that she would be wounded by an arrow at Orleans, but not unto death. The prediction was taken down in writing, and was fulfilled, as we shall see, a fortnight later.

Meantime a "Household," or retinue, had been appointed for the Maid of Domrémy, consisting of an Augustinian friar named Pasquerel, who acted as her confessor, a squire, and two pages. Of these Pasquerel must have been greeted with especial joy by Jeanne, for he had come straight from the town of Puy, whence he brought news of her mother, Isambeau d'Arc, and her two brothers who had gone there for the great yearly festival of the Annunciation, kept with special solemnity in that place; and he had talked to her brothers with such effect that the two young men were already preparing to join their sister on her march to Orleans, leaving poor Isambeau to return to Domrémy with a heart bursting with love and pride and fear for the girl she had nursed in the bygone years.

By the time they had left the town of Blois behind them,

her troop had been joined by a band of priests, who marched in advance under the banner made for her at Tours. This had been specially designed by the Maid, according to the directions given her, she said, by Saint Margaret and Saint Catherine. Upon a white linen ground stood the figure of the Christ holding the round world in His hands, with an adoring angel on either side. Below were inscribed the names, "Jesus, Maria."

The banner was generally upheld by the strong young arm of the Maid herself. "Take the standard from the hand of God and bear it boldly" her saints had told her, and Jeanne, with a girl's dread of bloodshed, was no doubt glad to exchange her little battle-axe for the banner, which would prevent her also from using the sword which hung at her side.

The whole army was "more like a religious procession than an army," for the priests sang hymns as they marched, and twice a day held a religious service beneath the sacred banner. By the strict command of the Maid, "no man might swear by aught but his *bâton*," or join in the singing "unless he were clean confessed."

Such, then, was the appearance of the force that arrived on the 28th of April on the south bank of the Loire, opposite the beleaguered city of Orleans.

The condition of this town, "almost the last barrier between the invader and the final subjugation of France," was deplorable. These huge towers, built by the English, threatened them from the outer walls; provisions were almost exhausted; the English, stationed in the camp between the Regnart gate and the river, had but to play a waiting game.

And yet perhaps the most curious part of the matter is that Orleans was strongly garrisoned, so strongly that her troops might well have been sufficient to drive off the English forces and to prevent them from building those threatening towers. The town was commanded, moreover, by Dunois, generally known as the Bastard of Orleans, a brave and popular young officer who had won the devotion of his people. Yet with all these advantages the place was doomed, and both those inside and those outside knew it but too well; for the French general and his men had alike lost heart, each success of their foes reduced their stock of hope and courage to a lower ebb, and made them less fit for the fight.

The first intimation that the English forces, under the Duke of Bedford, received of the coming of the Maid must have been the quaint letter dictated by her before she left Tours, and sent thence to the camp outside Orleans.

Jesus Maria

"King of England, and you Duke of Bedford, calling yourself Regent of France, you William de la Pole, John, Lord of Talbot, and you Thomas, Lord of Scales, who call yourselves lieutenants of the said Bedford, listen to the King of Heaven:

"Give back to the Maid who is here sent on the part of God the King of Heaven, the keys of all the good towns which you have taken by violence in His France. She is sent on the part of God to redeem the royal rights. She is ready to make peace if you will hear reason and be just towards France and pay for what you have taken. And you archers, brothers-in-arms, gentles and others who are before the town of Orleans, go in peace on the part of God; if you do not do so, you will soon have news of the Maid who will see you shortly to your great damage.

"King of England, if you do not this, I am captain in this war, and in whatsoever place in France I find your people I will make them go away. I am sent here on the part of God the King of Heaven to push you all forth of France. If you obey I will be merciful. And be not strong in your own opinion, for you do not hold the kingdom from God the Son of the Holy Mary, but it is held by Charles, the true heir, for God, the King of Heaven so wills, and it is revealed by the Maid, who shall enter Paris in good company. If you will not believe this news on the part of God and the Maid, in whatever place you may find yourselves we shall make our way there, and make so great a commotion as has not been in France for a thousand years, if you will not hear reason. And believe this, that the King of Heaven will send more strength to the Maid than you can bring against her in all your assaults, to her and to her good men-at-arms. You, Duke of Bedford, the Maid prays and requests you to destroy no more.

"If you act according to reason you may still come in her company where the French shall do the greatest work that has ever been done for Christianity.

"Answer then if you will still continue against the city of Orleans. If you do so you will soon recall it to yourself by great misfortunes.

"*Written the Saturday of Holy Week,* 1429."

One can but try to imagine the astonishment, not unmingled with blasphemy, with which the English general would read this letter, utterly naïve in its simplicity, boyishly straightforward in its frank confidence.

Dunois, meantime, had been told of the approach of the Maid with her advance guard of priests singing the *Veni Creator,* upon the village of Chécy, some five miles distant, between the town of Jargeau, held by the English, and Orleans.

At this spot they had crossed the river with the intention of marching into the city by the Burgundy gate, which was unguarded save by one English fort. But Jeanne's aim from the first had been, not to enter the city without a struggle, but to fight her way through the main camp of the English on the farther side of the city; and when she saw that her guides, taking advantage of her ignorance of the locality, had tricked her into what they thought a course of greater safety, her anger blazed forth. Her wrath, moreover, was justified still further by the fact that an adverse wind prevented the army from sailing up the river to Orleans, as was at first planned, and thus laid it open to the attack of Suffolk and Talbot, the English generals.

At this juncture she was met by that courteous knight

Dunois, who had come out from the city to meet her at Chécy. At once she faces him with the frank question:

"Are you the Bastard of Orleans?"

"I am, and glad am I of your coming," says he.

"Is it you," blazes forth the angry Maid, "who gave counsel that I should come by this side of the river, and not against Talbot and his English at once?"

"I, and others wiser than I, gave that counsel, and think it is the best and safest way."

"The counsel of God, our Lord," says she, scornfully, "is more sure and more powerful than yours. You think to deceive me, but you deceive yourselves, for I bring you better assistance than ever came to knight or city, the succour of the King of Heaven."

The courtesy and good-will of Dunois soon restored the Maid to her wonted high spirits and good humour. The wind changed to a more favourable quarter so that the convoy of provisions was able to sail in safety up the river to the city, which it entered "with no good will of the English" but with no opposition, as Jeanne had already foretold. Meantime, as the main army had to return to Blois to bring up another convoy, Dunois suggested that Jeanne should ride with him back to the city and enter by the Burgundian gate. Sorely reluctant to leave the soldiers whose hearts she had won to herself, the Maid at length consented, and either rode along the bank or sailed up the river with Dunois and La Hire, entering the city without the smallest opposition about eight o'clock in the failing light of an April evening.

One cannot wonder that the inhabitants of that beleaguered town thronged the streets to look upon the white vision of the Maid in shining armour, carrying her gleaming banner as she rode through the midst of them, and gazed at her "as if they had seen God descending among them."

"For," says an eyewitness of those things, "they had suffered many disturbances, labours, and pains, and what is worse, great doubt whether they ever should be deliv-

ered. But now all were comforted, as if the siege were
over, by the divine strength that was in this simple Maid
whom they regarded most affectionately—men, women,
and little children. There was a marvellous press around
her to touch her or the horse on which she rode, so much
so that one of the torch-bearers approached too near and
set fire to her pennon; upon which she touched her horse
with her spurs and turning him cleverly, extinguished the
flames, as if she had long followed the wars."

First she went to the Church of the Holy Rood, and
there made her thanksgiving for her safe entry into the
city, and then to the house of Jacques Boucher, treasurer
of the Duc d'Orleans, where she thankfully removed her
heavy armour and shared the bed of the little Charlotte,
the nine-year-old daughter of her host.

The second great step in the accomplishment of her
mission had been taken.

VIII

THE SIEGE OF ORLEANS
April 29–May 8, 1429

Travaillez! Travaillez! et Dieu travaillera!
(The favourite saying of Jeanne d'Arc)

THE arrival of Jeanne d'Arc in Orleans was the signal
not only for a great outbreak of loyalty and enthusiasm on the part of the harassed citizens, but for determined attempts on their part to drive the English from
their walls. It was all the gallant Maid could do to keep
them within bounds while she awaited news of the fate of
her letter to the English generals; for she never lost a
chance of winning the day by persuasion and warning
rather than by bloodshed.

Two heralds, Guienne and Ambleville, had taken the letter into the English camp; and presently the latter
returned with the news that his comrade was in the hands

of the foemen and about to be burnt for having been concerned with a witch and her affairs. The Maid heard the
information unmoved. "Return boldly to them," she said;
"they will not harm you, and you shall bring back Guienne
in safety."

Some say that this actually occurred, others declare
that the unfortunate herald was kept a prisoner, quite
against all rules of warfare, till the English retreat, when
he was found in irons in the deserted camp.

Meantime some citizens and men-at-arms under
Captain La Hire, roused by the sight of the Maid but dis-
regarding her plea for waiting until an answer to her letter
should be received, had made an unsuccessful sally from
the gate. It was left for Jeanne to conduct the campaign in
more dignified fashion by appearing that night upon the
rampart of La Belle Croix, which directly faced the English
garrison of Les Tourelles.

"Surrender in the name of God, and I will grant you your
lives."

So rang out the summons of the shrill girlish voice. She
was answered by foul insults, while the Captain, William
Glasdale, after a shower of evil names, shouted, "Milkmaid! If ever we get you, you shall be burnt alive."

And the Maid, brave enough in the face of danger, but
sensitive as the child she was to threats and insults,
weeps for her shamed womanhood.

Next day Dunois, the Bastard of Orleans, left the city to
go and meet the main army as it came from Blois. That
Sunday was a red-letter day for the beleaguered city, for
all that it was a day of peace. The citizens crowded round
the door of the house where Jeanne lodged—"they could
not see enough of her"—and threatened to break in the
door. When she hastened to appear before them they
prayed her to lead them at once against the English. But
she shook her head, and, mounting her horse, led them
instead down the narrow streets from one church to
another, dismounting and praying in each.

Later in the day she gave the foe their second chance to

submit without more ado. Riding through the Renard gate and down the road toward Blois she met a band of English men-at-arms whom she addressed in grave and dignified words.

"Surrender, and your lives shall be spared. In God's name go back to England. If not, I will make you suffer for it."

"Would you have us surrender to a woman?" they cried with coarse jeers; but they allowed her to ride back in safety after the deliverance of her message.

It seems, indeed, as though the rough men-at-arms had been impressed, in spite of their scorn, by that slight young girl who had so confidently addressed them, for when Dunois returned, two days later, with the convoy of provisions and the main army, no attempt was made by the English to hinder their progress. They remained fast within their forts, while Dunois, hastening to the Maid, brought her news that Sir John Fastolf, the victor of Rouvray, was marching upon the city from Paris with a large force. Eagerly the Maid begged that she might be told directly he arrived; and the courteous Dunois gave his promise and departed without further comment.

Weary with a long ride round the walls, Jeanne lay down on her hostess' bed to sleep, while her equerry, d'Aulon, thinking all was quiet inside and outside the city, stretched himself on a sofa in the room and also fell asleep. Suddenly he was aroused by a cry from the Maid, whom he found standing with anxious eyes and uplifted hand in the middle of the room.

"In God's name!" she cried to him, "My Voices tell me to go against the English, but I know not whether it is against their forts or against Fastolf."

Hastily d'Aulon began to buckle on her armour, for already there was a noise of cries and tumult in the street. "What is it?" cried the Maid from the window, and from the confused replies they discovered that an attack had been made, all unknown to her, on the English fort of St. Loup, and that the French were getting the worst of it.

"Hasten!" cries the girl to her page, for d'Aulon had rushed away to get his own weapons and armour. "Where is my horse? The blood of our people is flowing fast!" Springing on her horse and snatching the banner that the boy handed her from the upper window, Jeanne spurred off alone to the Renard gate, where d'Aulon and her page at length came up with her. Through the gate some men-at-arms were bearing a grim burden, one of the victims of this ill-considered assault. Brave as she was, the Maid, girl-like, sickened at the sight. "I have never seen the blood of a Frenchman flow without feeling my heart stand still!" she confessed.

It was the Maid's first actual fight. Hurriedly her scattered troops rallied round the white figure waving the gleaming banner, and, following her, returned in a breathless rush toward the bastille from which they had just been repulsed. For three hours the fight lasted, and all the while this child of seventeen, with her dread of bloodshed and fear of wounds, rode in the forefront, or, springing from her horse, stood on the edge of the moat in the midst of a hail of arrows and cannon balls, cheering on her men.

At length Talbot, the English general, brought a troop to the assistance of the English garrison; but by the time he came within sight, the fort was a smoking mass of charred wood, and the Maid was riding back to Orleans, victorious indeed, but heavy of heart because so many English soldiers had been slain in their sins.

The next day was the Festival of the Ascension, and Jeanne refused to permit further fighting; but she thought it a fitting opportunity to send a third and last message to the English, which ran as follows:—

> "Ye men of England, who have no right in the realm of France, the King of Heaven enjoins and commands you by me, Jeanne the Maid, to leave your forts and return to your country. If ye will not, I will make so great a noise as shall remain for ever in the memory of man: This I write to you for the third and last time, and I will write to you no more. *Jesus—Maria.*   JEANNE THE MAID."

To this she added a naïve postscript—

"I should have sent to you with more ceremony. But you keep my heralds. You kept my herald Guienne. If you will send him back to me, I will send you some of your men taken at the bastion St. Loup. They are not all dead."

This note was tied to an arrow, and as Jeanne mounted the walls she made an archer at her side shoot it to the English.

"Read! This is the message!" she cried.

A shout of jeering laughter greeted the missive, and a foul name smote Jeanne like a flintstone. Again she wept, but on her way back the smiles returned, and she told her companion that she had had "tidings from her Lord." All indeed was well with the sensitive soul of the Maid, while the Voice of the Divine Friend could be heard drowning the rude insults of her foes.

It was the attack upon the English fortification named Les Tourelles that finally established the reputation of Jeanne as an incomparable leader of men.

Les Tourelles was a stone fort consisting of double towers built on an arch of the bridge spanning the river, and was perhaps the most important point of vantage that the English held. On the Orleans side another arch of the bridge had been destroyed, and the towers were further protected by an outwork and a strong boulevard on the farther side of an arm of the river, crossed at that point by a drawbridge. The boulevard itself was protected by high walls and a deep ditch, so that the whole position was an exceedingly strong one and would give the Maid, in her own words, "much to do, more than I ever had yet."

Jeanne's first difficulty, however, was not with the English defences, but with her own people inside the city. The citizens were ready enough to follow her whom they firmly believed to have been sent them from on high; but the veterans of France, the nobles who had themselves failed and been repulsed by the English foe, thought the time was not yet ripe to take risks.

So, when the townsfolk crowded to the Burgundian gate, bent on recovering their lost stronghold on the bridge, they found that the Sire de Gaucourt had closed it against them, and was guarding it with his men-at-arms.

Dismay was spreading among the ranks when into their midst rode the white figure of the Maid, crying fearlessly to the old general, "You are a bad man to try to prevent my people from doing their duty. But they shall go, whether you wish it or no, and will succeed as they did the other day."

Her confidence and determination moved the old man at once. The gates were thrown open, and with a cry of "Come, and I too will lead you," the troops swept out of the city.

The river was crossed on a bridge of boats, and the attack on the outer fortification of Les Augustins was begun from many different points by means of scaling ladders. "In thick swarms came the French, attacking on the highest parts of their walls, with such hardihood and valour, that to see them you would have thought they deemed themselves immortal. But the English drove them back many times, and tumbled them from high to low; fighting with bowshot and gunshot, with axes, lances, bills, and leaden maces, and even with their fists, so that there was some loss in killed and wounded."

Baffled and disheartened, the citizen soldiers of Orleans fell back upon the island which stands in the midst of the river. At that moment Jeanne and La Hire, the French captain, who had crossed by boat with their horses, appeared on the scene, just as the English were charging the retreating Frenchmen in the hope of driving them into the river. "In God's name, forward! Forward boldly!" With such brave words rang out the voice of the Maid; a rush was made upon the defenders, and they were driven back helter-skelter behind the outwork of the Tourelles.

It was after this brief moment of triumph that Jeanne rode back to Orleans in chastened mood.

"Rise with the dawn to-morrow, and you will do even

better than to-day," she said to her men-at-arms, regarding them with grave and serious eyes. "Keep close to me; for to-morrow I shall have much to do, more than ever I had, and blood will flow from my body, above the breast."

Early next morning the attack upon Les Tourelles began, an attack which was to decide the fate of Orleans. Under the leadership of the young girl, who by this time they firmly believed to be of more than mortal stuff, the men-at-arms fought with the courage of enthusiasm; but the position was full of difficulty and the walls seemed impregnable. Close under them floated the white banner of the Maid, and ever and anon her clear voice sounded above the tumult. "Be of good cheer, *mes braves*. Do not retreat. The fort will soon be yours."

About midday, after a brief pause for food, the attack was renewed by means of scaling ladders. Jeanne was the first to seize one of them and to put it against the rampart. As she did so, an arrow pierced her shoulder, just over the right breast, in such a way that the shaft was half-buried in the flesh. Hastily her page and her confessor, Brother Pasquerel, carried her a little apart from the fray; and the Maid, seeing the flow of blood that followed the withdrawal of the arrow, wept bitterly like the girl she was.

Dismayed soldiers, crowding round her, suggested that charms should be used to stop the bleeding; but Jeanne would have none of them. She was dreadfully frightened and sure she was going to die; but she would rather that, said she, than do anything she knew to be contrary to the Will of God.

They took off her heavy armour, and dressed the wound with oil, and then mercifully left her for a little to herself. Presently she arose from her knees with her usual bright face and began to buckle on her armour. Her Voices had spoken words of comfort, and she was prepared to forget the smart of her wound and begin to fight anew.

But dusk was approaching, and she found Dunois, conscious of his weary and dispirited men, about to sound the retreat. "Sound it not!" she cried. "You will enter very soon, and the English shall have no more power over you."

He consented to wait a little, while his men rested and refreshed themselves; and meantime the Maid wandered up the neighbouring hill among the peaceful vineyards, that she might once more try to catch some echo of those heavenly voices that had encouraged her before.

All this time the standard of the Maid had been waving before the bulwark; and the Sire d'Aulon, one of the French captains, thinking to cheer his tired men, bade one of them try to carry it to the top of the wall. As he set off to do this Jeanne returned, crying with fresh energy, "Bring up your ladders. The English are well nigh done for."

Catching sight of her standard, she watched its course with brightening eyes. Crying to those about her, "Look and see when the flag of my standard touches the bulwark."

"Jeanne!" cried one of the lookers-on. "The flag touches!"

"Then enter, for the way is yours," she replied, and immediately rushed upon the rampart, followed helter-skelter by her host. The English, who had so lately seen her wounded and weeping, fled aghast before this unexpected attack and retreated to the wooden drawbridge by which they hoped to take refuge in the fort of the Tourelles itself. But the drawbridge was a mass of flames, and gave way beneath their feet, so that only a portion of the troops managed to cross through a perfect sea of fire, only to meet a new contingent from Orleans on the farther side.

Seeing the white, drawn face of their leader, Glasdale, the man who had replied to her former message with words of foul insult, the pitying heart of the Maid prompted her to cry:

"Yield thee, yield thee, Glasdale, to the King of Heaven. You called me an ill name, but I have great pity on your soul!"

But Glasdale with many another had met his doom, and

was choking out his last breath in the river beneath that flaming bridge of horror, while the Maid knelt weeping and praying for his soul on the wall above.

So Les Tourelles fell, and with it the English hopes of taking the city of Orleans. The joy bells that pealed out that night over the dark waters of the Loire sounded the knell of their hopes of victory in Southern France. In less than a week this country maiden of seventeen years had accomplished the feat which had baffled the wisest soldiers of France for seven long months, and had driven the foemen from the walls of the beleaguered city.

IX

The Chasse de Pathay
June 1429

Fille Dieu, va, va, va; je serai à ton aide; va!
(Les Voix)

THE following day, which was Sunday, saw a half-hearted attempt of the baffled English to recover their prestige by a fight in the open.

"In the dawn the English came out of their tents and arrayed themselves in order of battle. Thereon the Maid rose from bed, and for all armour wore a coat of mail."

But Jeanne was not to be induced to break the Sabbath rest without necessity. Says Dunois, now her admiring chronicler, "The Maid willed that none should attack the English." Instead she bade him set up in full view of both armies an altar, where Mass was celebrated with full ceremonies in the open air by the riverside. Both friend and foemen bent the knee in worship, and directly it was over, the Maid asked eagerly, "Which way are their faces turned now?" "They are turned away towards Meun"—(a town farther down the river).

"Let them go! The Lord will give them to you another time," she said; and so they were allowed to retire in orderly fashion upon Meun and Jargeau and the other towns still held by them upon the Loire.

Two days later Jeanne, though barely recovered from her wound, rode into Tours to interview the Dauphin. Her wish was to induce him to go at once to Rheims for his coronation, and thus to fulfil the divine command that was for ever ringing in her ears. But she found him listless and indolent as ever; stirred for a minute perhaps by her invigorating appearance, but content, as usual, to wait for a "more convenient time."

Banner in hand she met him face to face as she rode into Tours. Says an eyewitness, "The Maid bowed to her saddle-bow, and the King bade her sit erect; it was thought he would have liked to embrace her, so glad he was."

For a brief time all went well, and under the influence of Gerson, the supposed author of the *Imitation of Christ,* and Gélu, Archbishop of Embrun, the Dauphin could scarcely indulge in doubts and fears.

For the wise Gerson said of her, "If France deserts her, and she fails, she is none the less inspired," and the Archbishop solemnly declared, "We piously believe her to be the Angel of the armies of the Lord."

But the influence of less far-seeing counsellors prevailed in the end. The precious days slipped away, and in spite of the Maid's piteous cry, "I shall only last a year; take the good of me as long as you can," nothing was done. At length Jeanne could stand it no longer. Giving her quick boyish knock at the Council Chamber door, within which the Dauphin was holding one of his interminable colloquies with his advisers, the Maid marched in, and kneeling before him, cried, "Noble Dauphin, why do you hold such long councils? Come you to Rheims and receive your worthy crown."

"Is such the command of your Voices?" asked one of the councillors.

"Yes; they chiefly insist on it," she replied.

"Will you not tell us, in the presence of the King, the nature of the Voices?" he asked curiously.

She flushed up shyly, for a girl of seventeen is not wont to speak readily of sacred and intimate things. Then she said quietly, "I will tell you willingly if you wish to know."

"It is only if you are willing," said the Dauphin, who, with all his faults, was a gentleman, in a kindly voice.

"It is thus," she said. "When I am grieved because folk will not believe me, I am used to go apart and to complain to my Lord; and then I hear a Voice saying to me, *'Fille Dieu, va, va, va; je serai á ton aide; va!'* When I hear that Voice I am very glad, and would listen to it for ever."

And as she spoke she raised to heaven her shining eyes in a gaze which was full of hope and joy and clear vision of things unseen.

So presently she gained from the Dauphin a promise that he would proceed to Rheims if once the road was freed from danger and the English driven from the Loire.

Rejoicing to be free from the enervating atmosphere of the Court, Jeanne at once made her preparations for the campaign. It is as she was ready to start from the neighbouring town of Selles that we get a vivid picture of her, in a letter written to his mother by the Sieur de Laval, a Breton noble, who had lately offered his services and loyalty to the Dauphin.

"She left Selles on Monday at the hour of vespers. I saw her mount her horse, all in white armour except the head, a little axe in her hand. The great black charger was very restive and would not let her mount. 'Lead him to the Cross,' she cried; 'it stands on the road in front of the Church.' There he stood fast, as though he had been bound, while she mounted. Then turning towards the Church gate she cried in her girlish tones, 'You priests and people of the Church, make processions and prayers to God for us'; then turning to the road, 'Forward!' she said. Her unfolded standard was carried by a page; she had her little axe in her hand, and by her side rode a brother who had joined her eight days before. To-day d'Alençon was to join the Maid."

The last named was Jeanne's special favourite, as we

have seen, and she had hard work to get his young wife to let him go again to the wars. "Fear nothing, Madame," she had said reassuringly, "I will bring him back to you safe and sound."

And as they rode along the road to Orleans, with high hopes and intentions, while from time to time they were joined by fresh troops, new contingents hastily raised from the country-side by those who until now had given up all hope of saving their fair land of France from the English foe.

Those June days were full of triumph for the Maid. When before the walls of Jargeau, whither the English had retreated, the leaders who accompanied her were seized with their old disease of hesitation and delay, it was she who settled the matter by snatching her banner from the hands of the reluctant page, and, setting it below the battlements, cheered on her men to the assault. "Are ye afraid?" she cried to d'Alençon, aghast at this method of warfare. "Do you not know that I promised your wife to bring you back safe and sound? Forward, gentle duke, to the assault!"

She did not forget her promise. "Change your position! That gun will kill you!" she suddenly shouted to the young duke; and sure enough, a few minutes later one who had taken his place met his death there.

As she climbed a scaling ladder in her impetuous haste, waving her banner aloft, a stone crashed down from the battlements and struck her to the earth. There was a moment's pause among the soldiers, who had followed up her progress with growing enthusiasm; but in a moment she had sprung lightly to her feet, crying, "On, on, my friends. The Lord has given the English into our hands. Within an hour they are ours!"

The result of that brave speech may be seen in d'Alençon's own words.

"In an instant the town was taken; the English fled to the bridges; over a thousand men were slain in the pursuit."

Two days later the Maid announced that she "wished to

pay a visit to the English at Meun." Meun was taken, and Beaugency was deserted at the mere rumour of her approach, the English crowding into the castle, which at once she proceeded to besiege. And there befell an adventure which underlines not the least remarkable part of the Maid's character—her power of dealing wisely with men old in the ways of courts and camps, who would seem naturally to have been absolutely beyond her sphere.

Before Beaugency there had just appeared in full force the Count de Richemont, Constable of France, whom the hatred of La Trémouille, the King's adviser, had driven into exile, and into enmity with Charles, though he still held his troops in reserve to fight against the English if necessary. This great nobleman, having heard with contemptuous disgust of the exploits of this "milkmaid of Domrémy," had bethought himself that it was but fitting that he should put himself at the head of affairs now that things had come to such a pass, if only to put down an influence that must be due to witchcraft alone, a "thing he hated more than any man, and had burned more witches in France than any other of his time."

The news of his approach roused something like an uproar among the royalist forces. D'Alençon openly declared that he would throw up his command if Richemont were allowed to join the army; at which the Maid sprang upon her horse and called upon the captains to follow her, for she was "going to fight the Constable." D'Alençon and La Hire obeyed; others hung back, muttering, "There be some of us in your company who love the Constable better than all the Maids in France."

But Jeanne knew better than to throw away the chance of a good ally; there were other ways of "fighting" known to her, more sure of winning over a foe than by use of the sword. As they rode, they suddenly came upon the great man in full array, whereupon "the Maid dismounted and embraced his knees."

"Jeanne," he said in his rough but not unkindly tones, as he stood looking down at the young face upturned to his, "they tell me you want to fight me. Now I know not if you are from God or not; if you are, I do not fear you, and if you are from the Devil, I fear you still less."

"Brave Constable," she replied, "you have not come here for my sake, but since you are here, you are welcome."

In face of such frank behaviour, how could d'Alençon sulk in his tents? A friendship was patched up between him and de Richemont, and the flight of the English from that quarter was the immediate result of the increased strength of the allied forces.

It was while they were in full retreat toward Paris that Jeanne experienced her first battle on the open field.

The French were by no means eager for this, since, thus far, they had invariably met with defeat under those conditions; but the leader would not hear of delay or retreat. "In God's name, we must fight them; if they were hanging from the clouds we should still have them. This will be the greatest victory ever gained for the King."

It is said that the two armies, hidden from one another by the thick low woods of the plain of the Beauce, came upon each other almost by chance. A stag had been roused by the French scouts, and fled in its terror right into the English camp. Strong in their sporting instinct, the English raised the view-hallo and shot at the animal, thus betraying their whereabouts to the scouts of the enemy.

At once the French army prepared to rush upon the foe, though still with inward trepidation.

"What will be the issue of the fight?" d'Alençon asked the Maid. "Have you good spurs?" she answered with her ready smile.

"What! shall we turn our backs and flee?" cried the bystanders.

"Not so! But the English will not defend themselves, and you will need good spurs to follow up their flight."

She was right, as usual. The English fled before the determined onrush of the French; Sir John Fastolf, their leader, "who would fain have thrown himself into the fight," was obliged to follow them; and Talbot, the English general, was taken prisoner and brought before Jeanne, d'Alençon, and the Constable.

"You did not expect this when you got up this morning!" jeered d'Alençon, mindful of his English prison.

"It is the fortune of war!" replied the soldier.

Probably Jeanne's eyes were full of pity as she gazed at him. We know that she hated the aftermath of battle and siege. Says her page of her on the very occasion of the Battle of Pathay: "She was most pitiful at the sight of so great a slaughter. A Frenchman was leading some English prisoners; he struck one of them on the head; the man fell senseless. Jeanne sprang from her saddle and held the Englishman's head on her lap, comforting him; and he was shriven."

Had the Maid marched straight upon Paris after the *Chasse de Pathay,* it would seem as though all France must have been hers; but still she must be faithful to the Divine Voices which said that the King must be crowned at Rheims, and spoke no word of Paris. The hardest thing was not to fight but to stir up the Dauphin to action, and that was still to tax her utmost strength.

X
THE CORONATION AT RHEIMS
July 17, 1429

Consilio firmata Dei
(Motto upon the Coronation Medal struck for Jeanne d'Arc)

JEANNE's greatest difficulties came always by way, not of open foes, but of her pretended friends. It had been comparatively easy to chase the English headlong from the cities of the Loire; but it was no light matter to get the Dauphin to follow up the advantage she had won for him and to march to Rheims for his coronation.

Hastening to him after the battle of Pathay, she was received by him with the utmost courtesy and kindness. "I pity you because of the sufferings you have endured," he said, and with smooth words urged her to rest, to take things more calmly henceforth—in short, to take a leaf out of the royal book, and *laissez-faire!*

No wonder the impetuous Maid wept tears of sheer vexation at such conduct; and then, bethinking herself with that sound common sense of hers that the King's hesitation could only be due to want of confidence in her success, she set to work to cheer him.

"Have no doubt! you shall receive the whole of your kingdom and shall shortly be crowned."

Then she tried her best to effect a reconciliation between her royal master and the Constable, who had certainly earned some recognition for his good aid. Here, too, she failed. La Trémouille, the King's fatal genius, was at his elbow, and de Richemont, his ancient foe, was dismissed with ignominy. It is much to his credit that, instead of abandoning the cause of his ungrateful King, the Constable proceeded to carry on an energetic campaign in Normandy.

Meantime the Dauphin, now at Gien, held a long ten days' Council as to whether it was safe, or even expedient, to undertake the march to Rheims. At this Jeanne became really restive. When they pointed out the dangers on the road, she replied shortly, "I know all that!" and, with pardonable temper, "left the town in sheer vexation, and bivouacked in the field two days before the departure of the King."

At length, on the 29th of June, the army set out for Rheims and met its first important check five days later at the gates of the city of Troyes, held, and strongly held, by a hostile Burgundian garrison. This was a serious matter of debate for a King who loved to talk rather than to act. Should they push on, leaving a dangerous enemy at their back? Or should they attack a well-fortified and well-provisioned town?

So the councillors and captains talked on, revolving one plan after another, some of them wild enough, none of them practically convincing; and it was left to the Seigneur de Treves, no friend of Jeanne's in former days, to point out that the one great essential to these Councils had been carefully excluded.

"The King's expedition had not been undertaken because of the strength of his army, nor yet because of the probability of his success; but it had been set on foot at the urgent moving of Jeanne, who told him that he should be crowned at Rheims, and should find little resistance, since such was the will of God.

"If, therefore, Jeanne is not to be allowed to give her advice at the present crisis, it is my opinion that we should turn back."

So to the perplexed assembly presently enters the Maid, with her quick boyish knock and fearless gaze; and when the Archbishop of Rheims, as spokesman, points out the difficulties that face them and the advantage of retreat—

"Shall I be believed if I speak?" says Jeanne, with scarcely curbed impatience, turning to the King.

"If you have anything profitable and reasonable to tell us, you will be trusted."

"Gentle Dauphin, if you will wait for two days, Troyes shall be yours."

Cried the Archbishop in amazement, "Jeanne, we would gladly wait for six days if we were sure to get the town. But are we sure?"

"Doubt it not!" replied the Maid.

All that night Jeanne, having obtained a reluctant permission to act, toiled and organized and issued her commands. In the dusk of the morning her shrill girlish voice was heard by the citizens of Troyes, trembling within their walls, ringing out in the cry, "To the Assault!"

It was enough; the townsfolk, headed by their Bishop, issued from their gates and proffered their submission to the King; the city of Troyes was won.

Terror of the innocent Maid, whom they thought a fiend come straight from hell, seems to have brought the men of Troyes to their knees; for they proceeded to send to her a certain Brother Richard, a noted preacher of the place, in the hope that he would exorcise the Evil One.

It must have been a strange and almost ludicrous scene: the friar, in his rough brown habit, advancing with doubtful gaze and lagging steps upon the White Maid, whose bright young face, framed by the short straight hair, shone above her glittering armour. The rough crowd surges around, breathless with excitement; the friar advances closer, and suddenly flings a handful of holy water over her, to drive away the fiend. Jeanne's merry laugh rings out. "Come on and fear nothing! I shall not fly away!" she cries.

And immediately Brother Richard and the timorous citizens accept her, and soon are her warmest friends and admirers.

On she led the army, growing larger day by day, to Châlons, where the keys of the town were at once delivered up. Here she met a Domrémy man, and from their conversation we get a hint of the gnawing anxiety that she hid so well under her appearance of gay confidence.

"Do you not fear these battles, these sieges?" he asked. And she answered very gravely, "I fear naught but treason."

On July 16th she rode with the Dauphin in triumph into Rheims; and early the next day the coronation took place. An eyewitness tells in a letter how it was "a right fair thing to see that fair mystery, for it was as solemn and as well-adorned with all things thereto pertaining as if it had been ordered a year before." First, all in armour and with banners displayed, the marshal and the admiral, with a great company, rode to meet the Abbot who brought the vessel containing the sacred oil. They rode into the minster and alighted at the entrance to the choir. The Archbishop of Rheims administered the Coronation Oath; he crowned and anointed the King; while all the people cried, "Noël!"

"The trumpets sounded so that you might think the roofs would be rent. And always during that Mystery, the Maid stood next the King, her standard in her hand. A right fair thing it was to see the goodly manners of the King and the Maid."

When the Dauphin had been crowned and consecrated, the Maid bent and embraced his knees, weeping for joy and saying these words: "Gentle King, now is accomplished the Will of God, who decreed that I should raise the siege of Orleans, and bring you to this city of Rheims to receive your solemn sacring, thereby showing that you are true King, and that France should be yours."

"And right great pity came upon all those who saw her, and many wept."[1]

The task of Jeanne d'Arc, as given her by her Voices, had been accomplished, and up to that moment nothing but the most extraordinary success had been hers.

She had first seen the Dauphin in the early days of March, when, from the most sanguine point of view, the fact of his coronation seemed utterly remote. By the middle of July, in spite of the most wearisome and unnecessary delay and waste of time on his part, the road to Rheims had been cleared, France south of the Loire was saved, and the Dauphin was crowned King.

And now that her special work was done, Jeanne pleaded that she might go back to her mother in Domrémy. Her father she had recently seen, for he had come to Rheims, with her "uncle," and some other peasants from her native place, to see for himself the truth of the reports which must have seemed to him truly amazing.

He sees his little Jeanne, the girl he had threatened to drown rather than see her ride among men-at-arms, the chosen companion, not of the rough soldiers indeed, but of a King, of princes, dukes and noble captains. The present of money given him by Charles impressed him, but his slow peasant mind probably never quite realized the

---

[1]Andrew Lang, *The Maid of France.*

great work that his daughter had already accomplished. No doubt he told her, in answer to her eager questions, of her mother's longings and fears for her absent child; and that is why the tender-hearted Maid wept and besought the King that she might return to help with the sheep in the old home at Domrémy.

But Jeanne was by this time far too precious to be spared from active duty; and although she apparently realized that she was no longer fulfilling an actual divine behest, she was far too loyal, too enthusiastic, possibly also, too doubtful of the King's conduct unless she were there to incite to action, to shrink from continuing her work of delivering her country from the English. Certainly it was no worldly ambition that urged her on, for again and again she echoes, the same mournful little cry, "Make the most of me, for I shall last but a year!"

Yet, strangely enough, it seemed as though the fulfilment of the actual letter of her task showed the high-water mark of her success. From the moment of that consecration at Rheims, with its bright colours and flashing banners and clash of sword, with the sunshine lighting up the jewels of the crown and touching the head of the Maid as she stood with flushed cheeks and eyes bright with tears at the side of her King, a cloud began to creep over her young life, a cloud that was to grow darker as the months passed by, till it burst in thunder over a scaffold and a stake.

XI

THE SIEGE OF PARIS
September 1429

Renty! Renty! to the King of Heaven!
(Jeanne's war-cry before Paris)

THE blaze of light that shone upon the coronation scene had faded away. Jeanne, with many tears, had said farewell to her father and uncle, and left the former to return to Domrémy, his unaccustomed mind still ruffled and aghast at the strange sights he had seen in Rheims, but his toil-worn hand grasping very tightly the two tangible proofs, as far as he was concerned, of his daughter's success. For one was the purse of money that had been given him; and the other was a patent of exemption from all kinds of tax and tribute for the villages of Domrémy and Greuse.

He had seen his young daughter for the last time. When he next heard news of her, news of imprisonment and of trial, Jacques d'Arc remembered his former doubts and fears, and after sullen pondering forbade his weeping wife to name the girl to him from that time forth. The news of her execution seems to have broken his heart, for he died very shortly afterwards.

Meantime, Jeanne had before her the supremely difficult task of rousing a helpless, inert King to follow up the advantage she had won for him, and to advance upon Paris and the cities of the north.

Much time was wasted, and the Maid, in her young impatience, always hated delay. There was a fatal theory in the mind of Charles that if he could but secure the alliance of the Duke of Burgundy all would be well; and Burgundy, probably in contempt of his weakness, was ready enough to dupe him, to make a false truce, to encourage him to delay, that he might the more easily crush him in the end.

Even the Maid, though wary and on her guard against him, was inclined to strain a point to gain the allegiance of the Duke, and the more because, from this time forth, the directions she had received from her Voices began to grow vague and indistinct.

"Fear not, for God will aid you," was the tenor of their message in these days, which pointed to the presence of some danger, more or less definite, but gave no clear command as to what course to pursue.

On the very day of the Coronation she had written one

of her simple, almost boyish, letters to Burgundy. "Jeanne the Maid desires you, in the name of the King of Heaven, her true Lord, to make a long, good, and assured peace with the King of France. . . . All those who fight against his holy kingdom, fight against the Lord Jesus, King of Heaven, and of the whole world. I pray and beseech you with joined hands, fight not against us any more."

But it was not the letter of the Maid that brought envoys from the Duke to Rheims, envoys who were laughing in their sleeves as they laid their master's pretended proposals of peace before the King, and thus gained time to allow Bedford to enter Paris with his army, and Burgundy to pitch his camp in the neighbourhood of Amiens. A quick and decided march upon the capital, then undefended, would have brought it into Charles's hands. As it was he had lost his chance. The citizens had been inflamed against him by a report that he meant to order a general massacre; they turned to Bedford as their saviour, and fortified themselves against their King.

Meantime the persuasions of Jeanne had at length brought about a move. "The Maid," says a writer of the time, "caused the King to advance on Paris."

But at the first hint of opposition, without even approaching the important town of Compiègne, prepared as it was to surrender, the coward Charles "turned his flank and then the rear of his army towards Paris, and dragging with him the reluctant Maid, headed for the Loire."

His excuse was the chance of Burgundy's alliance, in which case he might surrender Paris to the King. Charles must have known the utter improbability of this; and Jeanne's feelings on the subject may best be gathered from a letter written, "on the Paris road," to her friends at Rheims.

"Dear and good friends, good and loyal Frenchmen, the Maid sends you news of her. Never will I abandon you while I live. True it is that the King has made him a fifteen days' truce with the Duke of Burgundy, who is to give up to him the town of Paris on the fifteenth day.

"Although the truce is made, I am not content and am not certain that I will keep it. If I do, it will be merely for sake of the King's honour, and in case they do not deceive the blood royal, for I will keep the King's army together and in readiness, at the end of the fifteen days, if peace is not made."

Her keen mind had grasped the hollowness of such truces: and she was one of those who most rejoiced when the retreat to the Loire was suddenly cut off by a combined army of English and Burgundian allies, so that they were forced to march back toward Paris.

It was while Jeanne was riding between Dunois and the Archbishop of Rheims on this road that we catch a remark of the Maid's that shows how far she was from merely seeking glory for its own sake. She had been joyfully pointing out to her companions the loyal nature of the peasants of the surrounding country. "Here is a good people! Never have I seen any so glad of the coming of the noble King. Would that I, when my time comes, were so fortunate as to be buried in their country!"

"In what place do you expect to die, Jeanne?" asked the Archbishop with curiosity.

"Where God pleases," she said very simply. "I know not the hour nor the place any more than you. And would it were God's pleasure that I might now lay down my arms and go back to serve my father and my mother in keeping their sheep; they would be right glad to see me."

White as snow, pure as a spring flower in her sweet simplicity as she rides between the hardened soldier and the worldly ecclesiastic, it is no wonder that the rough men-at-arms worshipped her, that the chivalrous young knights were proud to serve her.

But what was the English idea of the Maid who had already so effectively weakened their hold on France?

A letter to the King from Bedford at this time taunts him with leading about with him "a disorderly woman dressed as a man." In later days he speaks of the cause of the English defeats as being the "unlawful doubt the soldiers had of a disciple of the Fiend, called the *Pucelle,* that used false enchantment and sorcery. A woman of ill-character and a witch!"

It is seldom indeed that the eyes of the hostile world can pierce the disguise of outward things and discern the hidden saint; but in Jeanne's case the transformation of both appearance and character is almost grotesque, even in the eyes of one whose sight was dimmed by malice and resentment.

In the days that followed it was the great aim of the Maid to bring about an engagement in the open field; but the English kept fast within their earthworks and walled cities and would not risk an action.

"When the Maid saw," we read, "that the English would not sally forth, she rode standard in hand to the front and smote the English palisade."

But this had no effect, and, beyond some slight skirmishes, nothing was done until Bedford's army moved north into Normandy, when Compiègne was at once taken by Jeanne's host. This town, situated on the left bank of the Oise, and on the road to Paris, was in a very important position, and its surrender was followed by that of several others in that district. If only the King would have bestirred himself, it would have been an excellent base from which to have marched on Paris; but this seemed such a hopeless matter that, as usual, Jeanne determined to act on her own initiative. "Good Duke," she cried to her friend d'Alençon, "prepare your troops and those of the other captains. By my staff, if God wills it, I will see Paris nearer than I have seen it yet."

So these two, with their troops at their back, set forth on the long straight road, riding recklessly in their high spirits and hopes, and so reached St. Denys, the cathedral of which was held especially sacred by Jeanne, since it held the tombs of all the kings and queens of France.

Here they waited for a fortnight for the laggard Charles,

whose tardy appearance was hailed with joy by the soldiers. "She will lead the King into Paris if he will let her,"
they cried.

At first there seemed small chance of it, and we hear
that "the Maid was in sorrow for the King's long tarrying
at Compiègne; and it seemed that he was content, in his
usual way, with the grace that God had done him, and
would make no further enterprise."

It was only, indeed, after the Parisians had been given
ample time to strengthen their fortifications, and the
patience and courage of his own army were fast ebbing
away, that he gave permission to Jeanne to lead the forces
that were under her special direction to attack the city. He
himself, meantime, retired to Senlis with the main body of
the troops, and refused to show himself before the walls,
in spite of the urgent entreaty of d'Alençon and the Maid.

The attack upon Paris was made between the gates
of St. Honoré and St. Denys, about two o'clock in the
afternoon.

It was a hopeless matter from the first. The Maid knew
that the nobles who pretended to support her were less
than half-hearted in the fight. "She herself," she said, "was
determined to go further and pass the fosses." But she
had no divine directions on the matter to encourage her
brave heart; she could but do her best.

The walls were protected by two moats, the inner one
full of water, the outer dry. For all that long afternoon the
Maid stood on the ridge between the two, under a hail of
arrows, waving her tattered banner and crying her
favourite war-cry to the foemen on the walls, "Renty!
Renty! to the King of Heaven!"

Her own men seemed to have kept for the most part
well out of range of the firing, and so escaped with scarcely any loss; but a despairing note must have entered into
that girlish voice as the hours went by, and still they held
back from the attack. "She called out that the place was
theirs for the winning"; and they preferred an inglorious
post of safety.

Still, however, the Maid stood there alone with her
standard-bearer, in her worn and dinted armour, until, as
dusk drew on, she was wounded in the leg by a Burgundian arrow, almost at the moment that the ensign fell
dead at her side. They tried to carry her away, but she
would not go farther than a place of cover beside the
moat, from whence, through the gathering darkness, she
still gave forth her pathetic appeal to her men to charge
and "take the place that was theirs for the winning." They
would not hear her, and a blackness of discouragement
darker than the night fell upon Maid and men alike. Some
say the latter "cursed their Pucelle who had told them
that certainly they would storm Paris, and that all who
resisted would be put to the sword or burned in their
houses."

This is the report of one of those within the city who
could only have heard it from those outside, as he was
engaged on the following day in helping to carry off the
dead Burgundians for burial; but one can see in it a sign of
the growing jubilation of the foes, and the increasing dis-
loyalty among the forces of the Maid. Yet it was no fault of
Jeanne's that the attack had not been pressed to the point
of success.

"What a pity! What a pity!" is her repeated sigh, as
against her will she lets herself be carried back to the
camp. "If they had but gone on till morning, the inhabitants would have known."

Next morning, in spite of her wound, which was but
slight, she was up and ready once more for the fray. "I
shall not stir from here till Paris be taken!" she
announced. The downcast spirits of the men-at-arms were
stirred as much by her brave words as by the sight of a
small reinforcement under the Sieur de Montmorency,
come to "take service under the banner of the Maid."

Preparations were made, and the march begun to the
walls, when suddenly another little band of riders
appeared at their side. The cheers of the soldiers were
checked; these were no new allies but messengers from

the King, bearing peremptory orders that the siege be stopped at once. "The Maid must return to St. Denys."

The disappointment was heart-breaking. For a moment d'Alençon encouraged her by the reminder that he had constructed a bridge across the Seine, near St. Denys, from which a most advantageous position for fresh attack was gained. Alas! they were to find that Charles, in his determination not to fight, had ordered the bridge to be destroyed during the night.

It was a fatal policy, for not only was Paris hopelessly lost, but the main body of the army, not able to realize the criminal weakness and cowardice of their King, saw in this ignominious retreat nothing but a proof of the failure of the Maid to keep her promises.

And since we have the testimony of the English Bedford himself to the fact that hitherto the disasters of the English had been due "in great part, I trow, to the Pucelle, who withdrew their courage in a marvellous wise, and encouraged your adverse party and enemy to assemble themselves forthwith in greater number," it is clear that anything that belittled Jeanne in the eyes of the army was a fatal blow struck at the success of France.

When the retreat began in earnest, the Maid begged to be allowed to stay behind, probably in the hope of renewing the attack by means of the free lances she might attract to her side. In this she had divine authority. "My Voices bade me remain at St. Denys and I desired to remain; but the seigneurs took me away in spite of myself. If I had not been wounded, I should never have left."

Before she left the place, she one day slipped quietly into the Cathedral and laid her suit of white armour, now all dinted and tarnished by warfare, upon the altar of Our Lady. Was it, as some think, a sign that she had done her work and could hope no longer for success? Yet soon we find her once more in the front of the battle, cheering on her men as usual; and hopefulness was ever her strongest characteristic.

It is more likely that in her talks with her divine companions she had learnt the true secret of inward peace, and after offering up, under the emblem of her tarnished armour, her disappointments and discouragements, came forth again, strong in spiritual might, to do her duty whatever might befall.

XII

INACTION AND FAILURE
Autumn 1429–Spring 1430

Jeanne, Jeanne, tu seras prise avant la Saint-Jean
(Les Voix)

IT was a silent and downcast Maid that unwillingly accompanied the craven King on his return march through the fertile plains south of the Loire. Little by little the victorious army she had so blithely led melted away, until at Gien the last remnants of it were formally disbanded by Charles. In vain did Jeanne point out the need of fresh conquests, of relief that should be brought to those loyal towns that at any time now might fall a prey to English attacks. D'Alençon, her gallant comrade, was dismissed, and rode home, not unwilling, to his waiting wife, when he found that he could hope no longer for a repetition of those wild free gallops into the heart of the enemy's forces, with the bright-faced Maid at his side. One by one her captains faded away from the Court; "and thus," says the Chronicler, "was the will of the Maid and the royal army broken."

That autumn of the year 1429 was one of sad and gloomy inaction for Jeanne. She must have heard with bitter regret of the abandonment of St. Denys by the disheartened garrison and of the sacrilegious pillaging of the Cathedral, from which her own little suit of armour, so recently offered, was carried off by the English and sent in triumph to the King of England.

She must have heard with equal indignation of the

councils held daily within the walls of Paris, the Paris for which she had been ready to shed her last drop of blood, the "heart of the mystic body of the kingdom"; of the deliberating of the Duke of Bedford and the Bishop of Winchester with the Duke of Burgundy, whom the more powerful citizens claimed as the true regent of their city.

She must have heard with grief and dismay of the agreement made between them by which Burgundy was to hold Paris, not as regent, but as Bedford's lieutenant, in return for which he was to bring an army at Easter against those loyal towns within the Ile de France district which had held firm to Charles.

Meantime, Burgundy, having completed his all too easy truce with the latter, could retire in peace to Flanders, leaving Paris in the hands of his favourite captain, and regardless of the murmurs of the citizens there deserted by their idol, could give all his attention to his approaching marriage with a fair princess of Portugal.

No doubt the keen eyes of the Maid saw that had it not been for that ill-judged truce, the fruit of cowardice and inertia, this would have been the very hour for her crowning victory, and Paris, left almost unguarded, would have fallen an easy prey. But Charles would pay no heed to her words, being now absorbed in his reunion with the Queen, who at that time joined the Court and made her abode at Bourges. Here Jeanne was well lodged and looked after, and was apparently in high favour with the royal pair. As long as she did not insist on fighting, Charles was complaisant enough, liking indeed to spend money on her apparel and to dress her in fine clothes as became a Maid of France.

"He gave her a mantle of gold, open at both sides, to wear over her armour," it was afterwards declared, and at her trial they added that she was fond and proud of her gay clothes. What harm indeed if she were, seeing that, with all her success as a warrior, she was still but a simple-hearted girl of seventeen?

In one sense indeed these days of enforced idleness

were full of petty triumphs for the Maid, had she cared to realize the fact. The people of the town openly wore the medals struck in her honour, on which, at the Coronation, was engraved the motto, "Sustained by the counsel of God." And the Duke of Milan, writing to suggest that she should come to his aid in recovering his lost lands, called her "That very honourable and devout maid Jeanne, sent by the King of Heaven for the extirpation of the English tyranny in France."

Such things had no satisfaction for Jeanne amid the soul-wearying monotony of Court life. She avoided them whenever she could, stealing away to quiet little churches or the dim chapels of the great Cathedral, there to pray and to ask for clearer counsel as to her future.

Sometimes the women of the town would bring their rosaries to her, as she knelt with upturned face, that she might hallow them by her touch; but there was no mock sanctity, no pretence about the Maid.

"Touch them yourselves; they will get as much good from your touch as from mine," she would declare, with boyish directness. But she loved to scatter her largesse among the poor, and, as the good lady with whom she was lodged gave emphatic evidence in later days, "She was very simple and innocent, knowing nothing, except in affairs of war."

Then, almost suddenly, came news most welcome to the Maid. It had dawned upon the advisers of the King that the town of La Charité, on the Upper Loire, would be the future centre from which the English army under the boy-King, Henry VI, bound to arrive at latest by the following Easter, would harass the loyal French territory, while safeguarding Paris.

So La Charité must be taken, and Jeanne was the only leader who could be trusted to achieve that end. She had a companion in command, one d'Albret, but, as contemporary records repeatedly avow, she was officially recognized as "leading the hosts of the King."

It was a trifling drawback to the Maid that neither

troops, ammunition, nor money were forthcoming for this important attack. Bravely she set to work to raise the same in the neighbouring towns and villages, and the people, in admiration of her pluck and spirit, gave what they could, and added, over and above, a sword and two battle-axes for her whom they called the "Messenger of God."

Her first attack was on the town of St. Pierre-le-Moutier and was discouraging enough at the outset. Driven back from the walls, the hastily gathered troops fled in great confusion and, to the dismay of d'Aulon, the gallant gentleman who was at the head of the Maid's own military household, Jeanne was left beneath the wall with only four or five men, amongst whom were probably her two brothers.

Wounded as he was, d'Aulon managed to mount a horse and rode hastily back to her.

"What are you doing?" he cried. "Why do you not retreat with the rest? What can you do here all alone?"

To which the Maid replied in memorable words:

"I am not alone. I have fifty thousand on my side, and I will not retreat until I have taken this town."

To d'Aulon's mind the idea of the "spiritual hosts" that were so clear to Jeanne's eyes was inconceivable. "Whatever she might say she had only four or five men with her," he reported, "as I know for certain and so do several others who were looking on; so I urged her to retire like the rest. Then she bade me tell the men to bring faggots and fascines to bridge the moat; and she herself gave the same order in a loud voice."

And lo! the thing was done, to the great amazement of honest d'Aulon, who briefly adds, "And the town was stormed with no great resistance."

It reads like a miracle, but it was actually accomplished by human pluck and determination, though this was without a doubt sustained by that deep inner sense of fulfilling the Divine will which was the true secret of all Jeanne's success.

But before La Charité the cloud descended again upon the Maid. At her trial she implied that she had no divine encouragement, no "commandment from God" anent this town. She had, moreover, inadequate forces, neither money nor food for them, and her own private wish was to leave La Charité alone and concentrate her strength on the towns of the Ile de France, so as ultimately to secure Paris. No doubt she did her best, but her heart was not in the work, her soldiers grew impatient, and, after a month's siege, she was forced to withdraw from before the impregnable walls of La Charité.

Such a thing might well have happened to any general, seeing the difficulties by which she was beset—the bitter weather, the lack of food and ammunition, the discontented troops. But the crowd of ill-conditioned people by which the King was ever surrounded seized the opportunity of defaming the Maid, though the worst thing they could find to say of her was that she had promised her soldiers a victory which had never come about!

In order to discredit her Voices and divine intimations, her enemies at the Court had brought into prominence a certain Catherine, a rival who claimed to see actual visions, to which Jeanne, since her childhood, had made no pretence. This person told Jeanne she could find hidden treasure, and that "a lady in white" had commanded her to raise money from all the "good towns of France." To the ears of covetous courtiers such a suggestion was pleasant indeed, and Catherine was made much of, rather, perhaps, in order to make her outshine the Maid's reputation than for any real credit placed in her powers. But Jeanne quickly took her measure.

"When does your White Lady appear to you?" she asked, looking at her with steadfast eyes, and learning that she only appeared at night, promised to watch for her in the dame's company. The first night, overcome with healthy girlish fatigue, Jeanne slept soundly, and listened gravely in the morning to the reproaches of Catherine, who professed to have had a long conversation with the supernatural visitor. Then, having slept during the day, she kept close watch next night on the uneasy dame, who professed her certainty of the approach of the lady who never came.

"Go home and look after your husband and children," good-humouredly advised the large-hearted girl, who clearly saw through the woman's imposture. But Catherine must have her revenge on Jeanne.

She had advised the girl not to go to La Charité "because it was much too cold"; and when the expedition failed, she made the most of the fulfilment of her prediction, and found that her waning popularity had received an unexpected impetus thereby.

Baffled, disgusted by the mean ingratitude of the followers of her King, the King of whom even now she would permit herself no disloyal thought, Jeanne passed dark days enough amid that foolish, petty-minded Court. And ever when she sought counsel from above, the same answer was returned, striking cold dismay to her ardent young heart even in her moments of deepest resignation to the Divine Will.

"Jeanne, thou wilt be taken before the feast of St. John."

The notion of imprisonment, of grey stone walls and darksome dungeons was hideous to a girl who loved the free open air, who delighted in the healthy active life of the fields and roads; and she prayed with desperate energy that this might not be her lot, that if death were to come it might come swift and sudden in the midst of the exhilaration of battle or siege. But the only answer that came was an assurance that she would not be alone. "*Nous serons avec toi!*" And with this she was fain to be content.

It was but poor consolation to her in these miserable days of thwarted zeal and forced inaction, while Charles was wasting time in making truces with the Burgundians, that the King was pleased to grant her and her family a formal patent of nobility in recognition of her services. He was always very ready with such marks of esteem, for they actually cost him nothing and soothed a conscience that must sometimes have occasioned him vague discomfort; and no doubt the deed gratified the simple-hearted Maid as coming from the hand of the prince whom she never ceased to love and admire.

The patent of nobility runs after this fashion:—

"Charles by the grace of God King of France, in the perpetual memory of an event, and to glorify the high and Divine Wisdom for the many and signal favours which it hath pleased Him to confer upon us by the famous ministry of our well-beloved Maid Jeanne d'Arc of Domrémy, and which, by the Divine aid and mercy, we hope to see yet multiplied. We therefore judge it well to elevate, in a manner worthy of our royal Majesty, this Maid and all her family, not only in recognition of her services, but also to publish the praises of God, so that being thus made illustrious she may leave to her posterity the monument of a recompense emanating from our royal liberality, to perpetuate to all ages the Divine glory, and the fame of so many graces.

"Therefore be it known that in consideration of the services rendered to us and our realm by the Maid Jeanne and of those which we hope from her in the future we have by our special grace and wisdom ennobled the Maid, Jacques d'Arc of Domrémy, his wife Isabelle, Jacquemin, Jean and Pierre, the father, mother and brothers of the Maid and all her family and lineage."

There follows a list of the privileges conferred by such nobility, the freedom to hold fiefs, to carry arms, and all other prerogatives of nobles.

Did Jeanne's heart swell with pride under her robe of cloth of gold as she heard the great and high-sounding words of this decree? Did she not rather hear above the sonorous statement the persistent murmur of those other words, so simple, so significant:

"Tu seras prise avant la Saint-Jean."

XIII

THE LAST FIGHT
May 1430

*Mes enfants, je vous signifie que l'on m'a vendue
et trahie et que de brief je serai livrée à mort.*
(The prophecy of the Maid at Compiègne)

DURING the months that elapsed between the repulse at La Charité and the end of the truce with Burgundy many disquieting rumours reached the ears of Jeanne as to the state of her beloved country.

Paris was torn by plots and counterplots; the little towns of the Ile de France were constantly changing hands, to their own great misery and disadvantage; the royal city of Rheims was threatened by a siege, and appealed directly to the Maid for help.

"You shall not have a siege if I meet the foes," she writes to them with eager consolation, "and if I do not, shut your gates; I will soon be with you, and I will make the enemy buckle their spurs in haste."

Her hopes were still high; and indeed, from the English point of view, the army of the young Henry VI had much to fear in the forthcoming campaign from the result of her former energies.

Says Burgundy in his letter of advice to the English Council, written during that spring, "Owing to the campaign of July and August 1429 the French now hold many towns and fortresses on what was formerly the English side of the rivers Loire, Yonne, Seine, Marne and Oise. In these regions you will find no supplies. Paris is beset, and is daily in great peril and danger, for it had obtained supplies formerly from those towns that are now in the enemies' hands.

"To lose Paris would be to lose the kingdom."

He goes on to advise that time be not wasted in besieging Rheims for the sake of crowning the young King; and advises that the attack be concentrated on the town of

Compiègne, which, from its position as the most loyal town of the north, was able to hinder supplies from passing in to Paris, and to safeguard the royalist towns in the district.

This was the point of view of her enemies, and shows plainly that they realized to the full the difficult and dangerous position in which they stood. But Jeanne heard only of the misery of the people, of smoking villages and pillaged towns, of ruined crops and roads beset with desperate vagabonds, and chafed wildly at the golden chains that bound her to the Court when she was ready and longing to drive out the English foe and to capture Paris with one bold dash for victory.

At length she could bear it no longer. The Court was at Sully at the end of March when she made up her mind that to hope for official leave was useless, and so rode off with a little troop for Melun, a town that had been in the hands of the English for ten years until it had been given over in the previous autumn to the Duke of Burgundy.

Jeanne took this step in no moment of exultation or triumphant hope. She had wasted nerve force and vitality in the baffling atmosphere of the Court; she had knelt at the feet of Charles in vain; and she now rode from him for the last time not so much without his leave as without his direct prohibition. "*Laissez-faire!*"—it was the old old story as far as the King was concerned, and Jeanne, knowing her time grew short, determined to act as she herself thought best. But she could get no direction, no encouragement from her Voices as in the former days. When, at her approach about Eastertide, the town of Melun opened its gates to the King's men, she sought in that place another revelation, but it was of no exhilarating nature.

"As I was on the ramparts of Melun," she told her judges, "St. Catherine and St. Margaret warned me that I should be captured before Midsummer Day; that so it must needs be; nor must I be afraid or astounded, but take all things well, for God would help me.

"So they spoke, almost every day. And I prayed that

when I was taken I might die in that hour without wretchedness of long captivity; but the Voices said that so it must be. Often I asked the hour, which they told me not; had I known the hour, I would not have gone into battle."

Here speaks the true-hearted Maid, scorning to pretend she knew no fear of capture or death. Here was the highest form of courage, which "braves the danger nature shrinks from" when it was her duty so to do.

From Melun she rode to Lagny "because she had heard that they of Lagny made good war on the people of Paris"; and here occurred two incidents which were afterwards used against her in her trial.

Soon after her arrival she heard that the neighbouring roads and villages were being ravaged by a horde of bandit "Englishmen" or more likely Picard or Burgundian allies. Against these rode Jeanne and the Scottish garrison of Lagny, for nothing stirred the tender heart of the Maid more than the sufferings of the humble folk of the country-side. With some difficulty the men were taken or slain, and amongst the former was made prisoner a certain Franquet d'Arras, who was forthwith given over to Jeanne that he might be exchanged for a loyal Frenchman, landlord of a Paris inn, who had been imprisoned on a charge of treason by the Burgundians.

When news came that this man had either died in prison or been executed, Franquet was handed over to the authorities at Lagny, was tried, condemned and forthwith put to death. It was all fair enough under the circumstances, but the Burgundians raised a great outcry at the execution of a mere robber, who was, moreover, a prisoner of war.

They painted lurid and impossible pictures of the Maid as Franquet's executioner, and stored up the fact to be used against her when she fell, also a prisoner of war, into their hands. The other incident, which was used equally against her, was of a curiously different nature.

A child of three days old had apparently died before he could receive baptism, and, following a very usual custom, his parents laid him before an image of the Blessed Virgin in the church and asked all the maids of the town to pray to God that life might be restored to the child. Jeanne, always pitiful, and never far from church when not on active service, hastened to join the little group. "I went with the other maids and prayed and at last there seemed to be life in the child, who gasped thrice, was baptized; then instantly died and was buried in holy ground. For three days, as people say, he had given no sign of life. He was as black as my coat, but when he gasped his colour began to come back."

Thus to her judges, who asked insinuatingly: "Was it said in the town that you had caused the resurrection and that it was done at your prayer?"

"I asked no questions on the subject," answered Jeanne, with proud disdain.[1]

The taking of life, the restoration of life, both were turned and twisted into ropes to strengthen the net already wide spread about the hapless Maid.

It was in the first week of May that the recreant Charles discovered what Jeanne had known and acted on all along, and was able to announce openly to the people of Rheims that "the Duke of Burgundy has never had and now has not any intention of coming to terms of peace, but always has favoured and does favour our enemies."

Thus the time long wasted in pretended and impossible plans for truces came to an abrupt end, and open war was declared at last.

The chief object of the Anglo-Burgundian forces at this juncture (May 1430) was to capture Compiègne, the city that commanded the passage of the river Oise and the road to Paris. Their troops were concentrated some thirty miles to the northwest, and proceeded to make good their position on the northern side of the river. If Compiègne were taken, entrance into the Ile de France and so into Paris would be a matter of comparative ease.

---

[1]Andrew Lang, *The Maid of France.*

The Burgundians had already made themselves masters of most of the outlying posts on the northern side of the river, when Jeanne, hearing that the Duke of Burgundy and the Earl of Arundel were encamped before the city with a large force, exclaimed, "I will go see my good friends at Compiègne," and forthwith, in her accustomed way, started off headlong and rode rapidly by forest paths into the town. It was not her first visit to the place; she had stayed there for a few days on more than one occasion during these restless months, and had made "good friends" with the citizens according to her wont. There must have been some of these indeed who received her now with pitiful eyes and heavy thoughts; for fresh in remembrance was a strange little scene that appears to have taken place early one Sunday morning when the Maid had last stayed in Compiègne. Mass was over, when Jeanne was seen by the worshippers in the church standing with head bowed and face turned toward one of the pillars of the nave. The children, of whom there were many present, drew near and looked in awestruck silence on the sad young figure of her who was always their friend in joy or grief. A few older people joined them: possibly one of them inquired gently what ailed the Maid. Suddenly she faced them, crying out forlornly, "Dear friends and children, I have to tell you that I have been sold and betrayed and will soon be given up to death. I beg of you to pray for me, for soon I shall not have any power to serve the King and his kingdom."

Many years after Jeanne's death the story was told by two old men who at that time must have been young lads somewhat older than herself, and who had evidently been deeply impressed by her sad prophetic little speech. Had she any reason to fear and distrust those who should have stood her friends at that time? Or was it, we wonder, merely an echo of that grim warning sentence:

"Jeanne, tu seras prise avant la Saint-Jean."

It was just a month before that fatal date that Jeanne

rode gaily into Compiègne one bright May morning, laid her plans before Flavy, the Governor, heard Mass and visited the churches as usual, and then occupied herself in preparing the forces for a sortie upon the enemy.

Her plan was to make a sudden attack upon the village of Margny, held by the advanced guard of the Burgundian army under Baudot de Noyelles. This lay between Clairoix, held in force by Jean de Luxembourg, and Venette, where the English army lay, under Montgomery. If it could be taken, therefore, the forces of the enemy would be separated and a strong position achieved from which to attack the army of Burgundy, which lay about three miles beyond it.

The attack on Margny, at a time when most of the soldiers had laid aside their armour and were cooking their evening meal, promised well enough, seeing that the retreat of Jeanne and her men was covered by the bowmen who stood upon the ramparts of Compiègne. Quite easily the Maid reached the village and scattered the men at the outposts, but she was unaware that her movements were being watched by a little party of riders led by Jean de Luxembourg coming from Clairoix to visit Baudot.

In hot haste a message was sent for reinforcements, which rode up at the gallop and would have intercepted her then and there had not she gallantly forced them back twice along the causeway where she had drawn up her little band above the flat meadows that surrounded Margny. But by this time a party from Venette had come to the help of the Burgundians, and had driven her with her little body-guard down into the marshy fields. Still she returned, gallant as ever, to the attack, but her main body of soldiers, separated from their leader and terrified by the fast swelling numbers of the English, turned and fled helter-skelter back to Compiègne, with the enemy so close upon them that the archers on the ramparts dared not shoot lest they should slay friend and foe alike.

At first the Maid knew nothing of this, for the English horsemen of Venette had cut her little party off from her own troop; then at length, in desperation, d'Aulon and her brothers seized her bridle and forced her to retreat at the rear of the flying soldiers. Still she made a gallant struggle, charging back on the pursuers, shouting encouragement to her men; but the Burgundians were now in close pursuit, while the English spears could be seen gleaming in the dim twilight between Jeanne's little party and the crowd of fugitives which pressed upon the gates of Compiègne. Then, panic-stricken at the sight, de Flavy, fully expecting that in the confusion the foe would enter the city and make it their own, ordered the drawbridge to be raised and the gates to be closed, so that when Jeanne and her little company reached Compiègne it was to find their way blocked by a confused crowd of fugitives and foemen, all pressing hard upon the closed gates.

Her one chance now was to turn aside into the fields that surrounded the town and try for another entrance; but it was too late. The bright scarlet gold-embroidered cloak she wore attracted the attention of the foemen, eager for such a prize. Her few companions closed round her, fighting desperately, but to no avail. Surrounded by wild, dark faces, with open mouths yelling her own war-cry of "Renty!" (*rendez-vous*) she was dragged from her horse by a fold of her bright mantle, and brought to the ground in a *mêlée* of struggling horses and men and blinding dust.

"When asked to surrender," reports an eye-witness, "she said 'I have sworn and given my faith to another than you, and I will keep my oath!'"

Some say that de Flavy was guilty of treachery toward the Maid, and that it was of him she spoke when she talked of being "betrayed and sold." But it seems clear that the man could not well have acted otherwise. Jeanne would have been the first to assure him that his duty was to save the town at any cost, and to do this he was bound to sacrifice her safety.

So the Maid became, as has been well said, "a willing sacrifice for the people she had led." Most of them escaped; d'Aulon and her brothers and one other were carried off prisoners with her; and into the mingled glare and darkness of the Burgundian camp at Clairoix, ringing with shouts of triumphant delight, the weary young figure of the Maid of France disappears.

The exultation of the Duke of Burgundy over this capture, as shown in the letter written by him that night after a hurried visit to the camp to prove the truth of the report, was almost hysterical.

"By the pleasure of our Blessed Creator, the thing has so happened, and such favour has been done us that she who is called the Maid has been taken, and with her many captains, knights and squires. (This was a gross exaggeration of the facts.) Of this capture we are sure there will be everywhere great news and the error and foolish belief of those who were favourably inclined to her will be made known. We write you these tidings hoping you will have great comfort, joy, and consolation in them, and that you will give thanks and praise to our Creator who sees and knows all, and who by His blessed pleasure deigns to guide most of our enterprises to the good of our lord the King, and the relief of his loyal and good subjects."

Then the darkness of the night comes down on the weeping people of Compiègne, bewildered and distraught by the loss of her who had been their guiding star, and upon the exultant camp at Clairoix, where Jeanne was vainly trying to catch a whisper of her Voices to console her through the hours of that bitter night watch.

XIV

THE MAID IN CAPTIVITY
May 1430–January 1431

WHEN Jeanne d'Arc disappeared into the darkness of the Burgundian camp, it might well have been said by a poet of the day that the sun of France had set behind storm clouds of woe and distress for that unhappy land.

Perhaps the strangest thing of all about the matter is the very few people who seemed to care that such an event had actually happened. The English, it is true, made the most of it. Bonfires were lit in Paris, and a solemn *Te Deum* of gratitude was sung in Notre Dame.

And such loyalist towns as Orleans, Tours and Blois remembered the bright-faced Maid with regret and affection, for we hear that the inhabitants offered public prayers for her release, and in one of them, at any rate, the people to a man turned out into the rough cobbled streets, walking barefoot and singing the *Miserere* in penance for the sins that had brought this woe upon the land.

But what was the King about, or La Trémouille, or the forces inside Compiègne which she had led to the relief of that city? Did they attempt her rescue? Did they at least begin to open negotiations for her ransom as a prisoner of war? Nothing of the kind.

The men of Compiègne who bore the news to Charles and entreated further help to save the city were assured by the royal dawdler that he would speedily come to their aid; a promise that, it is needless to say, was never kept. Of the capture of the Maid he said nothing at all, being perhaps inwardly relieved that the strenuous enthusiastic spirit which had so often silently reproached him was likely to be quelled for the future.

Most sinister of all, alas! is the letter written to the men of Rheims by their Archbishop, in which he throws the blame of her capture entirely on the Maid. "She would not take advice but did as she chose." Then he goes on to say that the Court is now absorbed in a new prophet, a shepherd boy, "who says that *he* is commanded by God to defeat the English; and that this boy has declared that Jeanne has been suffered to be taken because of her pride and her rich raiment, and because she had acted after her own will and not followed the commands laid upon her by God."

So this young impostor, soon to show of what shoddy

stuff he was made and to expiate his folly by a violent death at the hands of the English, was readily received in the place of the Maid by the volatile Court, and Jeanne was almost entirely forgotten.

One Archbishop, he of Embrum, alone stood forth in her defence. "For the recovery of this girl," he writes boldly to the King, "and for the ransom of her life, I bid you spare neither means nor money, howsoever great the price, unless you would incur the indelible shame of most disgraceful ingratitude!"

But Charles cared nothing at all for the fate of the Maid who had given him the whole devotion of her loyal heart, and who, in her darkest hour of trial and approaching death, still held to it that he was the "noblest Christian in the world."

Jeanne had been led into the camp of Jean de Luxembourg on the eve of May 23rd. Two days later the news was known in Paris, and the very next day a courier rode forth from the city to the Burgundian bearing a letter written by the University of Paris, then an ecclesiastical rather than an educational body, and in close touch with the Inquisition, whose business it was to investigate all charges of sorcery or heresy. This letter, written without a moment's delay, suggestive indeed, in its almost indecent haste, of the temper of a cat who has long watched the hole of a mouse and sees its victim at length in the grip of a passing grimalkin, demanded that "the said Jeanne be brought as prisoner before us with all speed and surety, being vehemently suspected of various crimes springing from heresy, that proceedings may be taken against her before and in the name of the Holy Inquisition and with the favour and aid of the doctors and masters of the University of Paris, and other notable counsellors present there."

A formidable array indeed to consider the matter of one little unlearned maiden who could neither read nor write. And the strangest thing of all is that she, most devout and pious of the daughters of the Catholic Church, should be the object of that Church's suspicion and distrust. We can but find one explanation. Jeanne was to find no royal road to the bliss that awaited her in a future life, and she was spared no humiliation in this one; and just as of her Divine Master it was said by His own people, "He is a Samaritan and hath a devil," so by her own countrymen and those of her own most fervent Faith was she to be judged a heretic and a witch.

The Maid was, of course, far too valuable a prisoner to be handed over in this summary fashion to the ecclesiastical authorities. After being kept for a few days in the camp at Clairoix, she was sent by de Luxembourg to his strong castle of Beaulieu, where she was treated as a prisoner of war and allowed for a while to retain d'Aulon as her squire.

Here she remained for a fortnight, refusing steadfastly to give her parole, and determined indeed to make her escape at the earliest opportunity. She had as yet lost none of her fine courage, though harassed by depressing reports of the condition of her "good friends" at Compiègne.

"That poor town of Compiègne that you loved so much," said d'Aulon to her one day; "by this time it will be in the hands of the enemies of France."

"Not at all!" flashed forth the Maid; "the places which the King of Heaven has put in the hands of the gentle King Charles through me will not be retaken by his enemies."

A few days later, perhaps because the dread of this weighed upon her mind, she made her first effort to escape, slipping in her girlish slightness between two of the laths which were nailed across the door of her room, and hoping, it would seem, to lock her warders up within the guard-room, and so be free. But she was caught by a gaoler in the passage, and taken back at once.

Probably because of this attempt, she was sent to the Castle of Beaurevoir, forty miles away, where she remained till the end of September. In some ways this might have been the most bearable part of her captivity, for she was in the charge of three good and gentle ladies, the aunt and wife of Jean de Luxembourg, and his step-daughter Jeanne de Bar.

All good women fell in love with the Maid at first sight, and these were no exceptions to the rule. Woman-like, they wished to pet her, to dress her in soft feminine attire, and looked with horror on her rough, travel-stained boy's clothes. But on this point Jeanne was firm. "She could not do this without leave from God," she said. "It was not yet time."

The whole question of the dress was made much of at her trial, as we shall see. One of her most understanding chroniclers says she regarded man's attire as the "symbol of her resolute adherence to her mission." It is more than likely too that she knew it was the best protection she could have among rough men-at-arms, some of whom were still her gaolers, even in the peaceful shades of Beaurevoir. Besides, the idea of escape was always present in her mind, and more so than ever here, where disquieting rumours came very frequently concerning the siege of Compiègne.

A report that, if the city were taken, all those over seven years of age were to be massacred seems to have made her desperate. She determined to make a leap for liberty from the tower where she was imprisoned, and this in spite of her Voices who bade her "bear these things gladly, since God would help them of Compiègne." With girlish impatience she replied, "Since that is so, I too would be with them." Then came a mysterious intimation that she would not be delivered "till she had seen the King of England." "I have no wish to see him," she cried, "and I would rather die than be in English hands."

The thing preyed upon her mind. "I would rather die than live after such a massacre of good people, and that was one of the reasons for my leap from the tower of Beaurevoir." So she told her judges, and leap she certainly did, and falling about sixty feet was picked up stunned and bleeding, but with unbroken bones.

She came to herself very sad and humble. She said she "was comforted by Saint Catherine who bade her confess and pray God's pardon for having leaped." But what cheered her most was the intimation from the same source that Compiègne should have succour before Martinmas.

This actually happened, and Compiègne remained in the King's hands.

There now comes upon the scene the man who was to be the Maid's worst enemy, Cauchon, Bishop of Beauvais. From the first, as representative of the University of Paris rather than of the Catholic Church in that part of France, Cauchon had set himself to track down the Maid to her destruction. It was his representations that caused her to be removed from her kind guardians at Beaurevoir, and that stirred the English to offer blood-money to de Luxembourg as the price of "Jehanne la Pucelle, said to be a witch, and certainly a military personage, leader of the hosts of the Dauphin."

The money, six thousand francs, was raised from a tax upon the estates of Normandy, and paid over by Bedford to Luxembourg, who turned a deaf ear to the earnest prayers of his womenkind on Jeanne's behalf.

For a brief space, while these transactions were being carried on, the Maid, now imprisoned at Crotoy, had great comfort in the spiritual administrations of a priest, one Nicolas de Guenville, a fellow-prisoner and loyalist Frenchman, who, after hearing her confession and giving her Holy Communion, declared her to be a most devout Catholic Christian.

From Crotoy she was passed over into the hands of the English, and, in spite of the outcry of the Paris doctors of divinity, taken by them in November to Rouen and imprisoned in a strong and ancient castle of the days of Philip Augustus. Here she was placed "in a dark cell, fettered and in irons." No kindly women were now her guardians, but rough and brutal English archers, to whom she was merely a witch who had brought disgrace upon their

arms, and who thought it no shame to bully and ill-use a
helpless young girl.

The Earl of Warwick was in command of the Castle, and
the most absurd precautions were taken by him to prevent
any attempt at escape. Indeed, the whole story of this part
of her imprisonment would lead us to think that it was
some wild and savage beast they needed to cage and bar
and fetter rather than a child of eighteen, already weakened by six months of captivity. All hope of escape must
have now faded from her mind, but one can but think she
still expected a rescue, if not a ransom, from those for
whom she had fought so well in the days of freedom.

Only a few leagues away, at Louvain, her old comrade
La Hire was stationed, and he was joined there by Dunois,
her friend and favourite, a few months later. But we get no
hint of any attempt at rescue from there, while from the
south, where Charles was still dawdling about from castle
to castle, not the smallest sign of interest, far less of pity
or distress on her account, is to be seen. It was as though
France, her "bel pays," for which she had fought and striv-
en and bled, had utterly forgotten her very existence.
Who can say that, if she ever realized the fact, it was not
the bitterest drop in that cup of sorrow which she was yet
to drain to the dregs?

The story of that five months' captivity in the castle of
Rouen is even more tragic than its sequel.

A citizen of Rouen, who managed to gain admission to
her cell, saw her chained by the feet to a heavy log of
wood, and was told that, when asleep, she was ironed by
the legs with two pairs of heavy fetters locked to the bed.
She still wore her boy's clothes, but in place of the courteous d'Aulon, her room was shared day and night by
three English archers, while two more kept guard outside.

Even the horrors of the actual trial must have been a
welcome respite from such an existence. For Jeanne, we
must realize, had always shown herself singularly self-
respecting and instinctively refined in nature; and the
rude jests, the coarse laughter, nay, the evil advances of

these low-class soldiers, not to speak of their constant presence, must have been nothing less than the extremity of torture to her pure and modest spirit.

But this was not all that the Maid had to suffer before the actual trial began. Other visitors than the inquisitive citizen of Rouen were to enter her dark cell. One of these was no less a person than Jean de Luxembourg, her captor, who was brought into the place by the Earl of Warwick, together with another English lord, apparently only with the intention of harassing and worrying the girl.

De Luxembourg pretended he had come to ransom her. "Jeanne," said he, with mock gravity, "I will have you ransomed if you will promise never to bear arms against us any more."

But the Maid's spirit was not yet broken.

"It is well for you to jest," she flashed back, "but I know you have no such power. I know that the English will kill me, believing, after I am dead, that they will be able to win all the kingdom of France; but if they were a hundred thousand more than there are, they shall never win the kingdom of France."

Enraged at these words, the English lord who accompanied the Duke drew his dagger and would have struck her, had not Warwick intervened, not from any instinct of humanity, one fears, but to reserve her for a darker fate.

Another and more dangerous visitor was one who came to her as a fellow-countryman from the marches of Lorraine, and a prisoner like herself. By an act of charity so unusual that Jeanne might well have suspected treachery, her guards left the girl alone with this man, in order that they might talk freely together. He led her on with ease to converse of the old days at Domrémy, that seemed now so remote, though it was but two years since she had left the place, of the oak wood, and the pleasant meadows and of her Voices as they had been heard by her in those spots.

His kind face soothed and encouraged the girl, especially when he spoke of her approaching trial, telling her that no harm could come to her. She little knew that he was a spy in the pay of Cauchon, in reality a canon of Rouen Cathedral, and that every word of her conversation with him had been recorded by the Bishop himself and the Earl of Warwick, who, with two notaries, had been listening at a peep-hole contrived in the wall of her cell.

One marvels that the very innocence of her remarks did not touch their hearts. One of the notaries indeed strongly protested against evidence obtained in this way and refused to record it. That her judges should stoop to such a trick shows the weakness of their case against the Maid.

XV

THE PUBLIC TRIAL
February 1431

Passez-outre!
(Jeanne's exclamation at the Trial)

AT Bonsecours there stands a statue of the Maid by Barrias, named "Jeanne d'Arc, prisonnière." It shows her wearing armour, which is incorrect enough, but one scarcely notes the fact, so is the attention centred on the pitiful manacled hands, the boyish attitude, and the fine young head thrown back from the shoulders as though in amazed protest at the way the world is treating her. The soft lips droop pathetically, the wide-open eyes are full of simple indignation. "What have I done unto you that you should do this to me?" she seems to be asking, and reminds us yet once again of that far-off cry down the ages of the Christian world:

"Oh my people, what have I done unto thee? And wherein have I wearied thee? Answer Me."

Three months had elapsed since Jeanne had passed beyond the dark portals of Rouen Castle, months of terror, of hideous companionship far worse than loneliness, of deprivation of the sacraments, of dread for the future.

At the end of February began that extraordinary trial, in which we find the chief ecclesiastics of the realm, the University of Paris, as represented by the Bishop of Beauvais, the English Council, with the child-King, Henry, as its nominal head, all arrayed against a young peasant girl, who "conducted her own case," as we say, whose only defence was her own free, simple speech.

Her actual judge was the Bishop of Beauvais, to whom she was passed over, after long deliberation, by the English, who, however, claimed her as their prisoner of war even if she were acquitted by him. The document by which this was effected gives the offences with which Jeanne was charged, and on account of which she was claimed by the Ecclesiastical Court.

"Henry, by the grace of God, King of France and England, to all who shall see these present letters, greeting: It is sufficiently well known how, some time ago, a woman who caused herself to be called Jeanne the Maid, forsaking the garments of the feminine sex, did, against the Divine Law, clothe and arm herself in the fashion of a man; did do and commit cruel acts of homicide, and gave the simple people to understand that she was sent from God, and had a knowledge of His divine secrets; together with many other perilous doctrines, very scandalous to the Catholic faith.

"In pursuing these deceits and exercising hostility towards us she was taken armed before Compiègne, and has since been brought prisoner to us. And because she is by many reputed as guilty of divers superstitions, false teachings and other treasons against the Divine Majesty, we have been earnestly required by the reverend father in God, our friend and faithful counsellor, the Bishop of Beauvais, and also exhorted by our very dear and well-beloved daughter, the University of Paris, to surrender her to the said reverend father that he may proceed against her according to the rule and ordinance of the divine and canon laws. Therefore is it that we, in reverence and honour for the name of God, and for the defence

and exaltation of the holy Church and Catholic faith, do
devoutly comply with the requisition of the reverend
father in God, and the exhortation of the doctors of the
University of Paris."

For insincerity and humbug this precious document
would be hard to beat. Not a man, woman, or child in
Rouen but knew that the sole reason for all this bitter
enmity against Jeanne was that she, a mere girl, had
revived a dying cause, relieved besieged towns, beaten
the English off the battlefield, and put to shame the might
of English arms. But this must not be said aloud; it would
be far more dignified to put the matter on high religious
grounds, and in the name of faith and religion pass her
over to Holy Church to be tried as a heretic. Yet, lest she
should escape the net thus cunningly woven for her, the
document contained a further clause that speaks for
itself:

"Nevertheless, it is our intention, if the said Jeanne be
not convicted nor attainted of the crimes above named,
nor of any of them, nor of others concerning our holy
faith, to have her and take her again to ourselves."

It is remarkable that the special court for the judgment
of heresy, the Holy Office, usually known as the
Inquisition, was exceedingly reluctant to be drawn into
the matter, and the Grand Inquisitor openly pleaded business elsewhere when called upon to assist the Bishop of
Beauvais. But the latter was fully equal to carrying out
what he gleefully called a "beautiful trial"; and it would be
a hard matter for this most innocent of criminals to evade
his toils.

For months his emissaries had been following the foot-
steps of the Maid from her very birth, prying here, ques-
tioning there, gathering all kinds of gossip and idle
chatter, not at all averse from bringing forward as witnesses miserable creatures who from envy and malice
were willing to defame the name of this most upright of
soldier maids.

A crowd of canons, doctors and masters of the University, priests and notaries, were the assistants of the Bishop—even a representative of the Holy Office was brought forward at the last minute; and when all was ready, the priest, Jean Massieu, was sent to read to the prisoner in her cell the mandate requiring her to appear "on the morrow, at eight o'clock in the morning, before the court appointed to try her for the heresies and other crimes of which she was accused and defamed."

Her reply shows something of the old spirit, undimmed by three long months of fetters and close confinement.

"Let there be present as many reverend men who are on the side of the French king as there are on the side of the English; and let me have a learned clerk to speak for me; then will I obey it," said she. And when they refused this, she begged with more humility that at least she might be allowed to hear Mass before the trial. This was also denied her, on the score that she still adhered to "an unbecoming dress."

On a cold February morning (Feb. 21st, 1431) the Maid was brought into the chapel of Rouen Castle, where the trial was to be held. Very slim and boyish she looked as she walked up the crowded aisle, dressed in a page's black suit, with her hair cut short to her neck.

Knowing nothing of legal procedure, and probably quite unaware that the trial was to be for her a question of life and death, Jeanne's first glance round the court must, nevertheless, have filled her with vague foreboding and put her on her guard. For when Cauchon, Bishop of Beauvais, warned her, in gentle tones but with an undercurrent of malevolence that was not hid from her clear young gaze, to "speak the full truth concerning those things of which you are accused respecting the faith," she replied with unwonted caution, "I do not know on what subjects you will question me. Perhaps you will ask me such things as I shall not be able to answer."

"You must swear," repeated the Bishop, "to speak the truth on all that shall be asked you concerning the faith."

"I will swear to tell you the truth of my father and

mother and of what I have done since I came into France; but of the revelations made to me on the part of God, I will not tell them, nor of the secret I told to my King. I will not speak about them if you cut my head off; for I have been warned by my 'Counsel.'"

It was thus she always spoke of her Voices, and at the mention of them such a stir was made in the court that some of her words were lost. Possibly her attitude of defiance went against her, but in face of such obviously hostile judgment, it was inevitable that she should try to guard herself by whatever reserve was possible. Finally, however, she knelt down and took the oath upon a copy of the Gospels that she would tell the truth on all matters concerning her faith. But again and again the spirit of girlish defiance broke out.

Asked to say her *Paternoster* to the Bishop, she flatly refused, "unless he would hear her confession, then she would say it gladly." She evidently was very sore at heart that she, a loyal daughter of the Church, should be refused the Sacrament of Penance, and took this way of showing her resentment.

Again, before the session ended for that day, the Bishop gave a solemn charge that she should not try to escape from her prison, on pain of being declared convicted of the crime of heresy.

"I do not accept that. I will give no parole," she flashed back at him. "So that if I do escape no one can blame me for having broken faith, for I never gave it to anyone."

Then came a very natural and piteous little complaint of her heavy fetters, to which she received the severe reply that she had several times tried to escape, and for that reason she was chained, that she might be kept more securely.

"It is true that I wished and always shall wish to escape," she said. "It is lawful for all prisoners to do that."

At that she was conducted back to prison, under strict directions that she was neither to see nor speak to anyone.

The proceedings of the next day were held in the Castle hall, for the chapel was found to be far too small for all those who wished to be present. But Jeanne, as she passed the door, had asked, "Is not the Body of Our Lord in that chapel?" and had knelt in prayer, while Massieu, her guardian, looked the other way. Even that was made a cause of offence, and Massieu was sternly rebuked for allowing this pious young daughter of the Church to gain a moment of consolation from the worship of her Master.

This day began with a close and detailed examination as to the facts of her life at Domrémy. The questions were purposely confused and intricate in order to entrap the Maid; and her answers were interrupted, misinterpreted, and disputed, till the brain of a well-trained lawyer might well have reeled under such an ordeal. It was, moreover, the Lenten season, and Jeanne had not tasted food since the one meal of the previous day.

Yet she never seems to have wavered or become confused. With perfect straightforwardness she told her simple story, only showing impatience when obviously silly questions were put to her, such as:

"How could she see the light in which her visions appeared if it was at the side, and not in front?"

Or unnecessary and impertinent queries as to whether she had made her Holy Communion at other feasts besides Easter, or whether she thought it right to fight on a Holy Day.

"*Passez-outre!*" (pass on to something else) she replies to all such questions, with pardonable asperity.

Her self-possession is as amazing as her clear-headedness. As one of her biographers well says, she might have been "a princess, answering frankly, or holding her peace as seems good to her, afraid of nothing . . . without panic and without presumption. The trial of Jeanne is indeed almost more miraculous than her fighting; a girl of nineteen, forsaken of all, without a friend."[1]

---

[1]Mrs. Oliphant, *Jeanne d' Arc.*

On the third day a fresh altercation about her oath to answer truly every question she was asked, began.

The record says, "We required of her that she should swear simply and absolutely without adding any restriction to her oath. To which she answered, 'By my faith, you may well ask me such things as I will not tell you: and on some things perhaps I shall not answer truly, especially on those that touch my revelations; for you may constrain me to say things I have sworn not to say.' Then to the Bishop she said fearlessly, 'I tell you, take great heed of what you say, you that are my judge. You take a great responsibility in thus charging me. I should say that it is enough to have sworn twice.'"

They pressed her again on this point, and she replied that she was ready to speak truth on "what she knew"; and when again they urged her, she exclaims with her usual boyish impatience, "Pass on to something else!" (*Passez-outre!*)

They asked her about her Voices, questions minutely detailed, unnecessarily confusing; to which she replied clearly enough. But when they pressed her as to the revelations given, she would not answer, save that she had revelations touching the King, which she would not tell, and that she was forbidden to speak of these. They asked if she had heard her Voices recently, and she replied that they had been with her on the previous night and had spoken much to her for the good of the King, which she would be glad to let him know.

They tried to discredit her visions by asking if it was by their advice she tried to escape from prison; which she took up shortly and sharply with the rejoinder:

"I have nothing to say to you on that point."

"Did you see anything besides the Voice?" asked the Bishop. To which she answered:

"I will not tell you all; I have not leave; my oath does not touch on that. My Voice is good and to be honoured. I am not bound to answer you about it."

She may well have felt by instinct that the strangely intimate nature of her vision would be profaned by discussion in the midst of that sneering, prejudiced court.

They next pressed her about her early associations with the "Fairies' Tree," and the Oak Wood of Domrémy, in the hope of showing that she had from childhood been associated with magic and sorcery. The frank and simple information given in reply suggests that Jeanne did not even suspect the purport of these questions. She certainly made no effort to hide or disguise the truth.

"What have you to say about a certain tree that is near to your village?"

"Not far from Domrémy is a tree that they call the 'Ladies' Tree,' others call it the 'Fairies' Tree.' Near by is a spring to which people sick of the fever come to drink. I have seen them come thus myself; but I do not know if they were cured. It is a beautiful tree, a beech. I have sometimes been there to play with the young girls, and to make garlands for Our Lady of Domrémy. Often have I heard the old folk—not of my family—say that the fairies haunt this tree. Whether it is true, I do not know; as for me I never saw them.

"I have seen the young girls putting garlands on the branches of this tree, and I myself have sometimes put them there with my companions; but ever since I knew I had to come into France, I have given myself up as little as possible to these games and distractions. Since I was grown up I do not remember to have danced there. I may have done so formerly with the other children; I have sung there more than danced."

Surely the frank admission must have proved even to those prejudiced minds that here they had to deal with no witch maiden, but with a simple village girl, recalling her childish amusements with evident effort, for they had receded, oh! so far, since she had taken up the banner at her Lord's command.

Suddenly, at the end of this long wearisome day, they asked her if she wished to have a woman's dress.

For a moment her heart leaped up. Did this mean

release? "Bring me one to go home in, and I will gladly use it," she said; then realizing the hopelessness of that idea she quickly added, "No, I prefer this, since it pleases God that I should wear it."

The question of her boy's dress was brought up again later. They tried to force from her an admission that she wore it at the suggestion of Robert de Baudricourt; and when she gave a flat denial, they asked if she herself thought it was well to dress in male attire. She replied firmly that she had done nothing in the world but by the order of God.

So the long days followed on another, full of weary, pointless interrogations, repetitions, absurd and trifling details. The marvel is that the Maid bore them so well, and showed such spirit, such power of repartee, when she must have been physically and mentally wearied in the extreme.

Thus, when they asked her if her Saints wore rings, she replies with contempt, "I know nothing about it," and then, turning sharply on the Bishop, she adds, "But you have one of my rings; give it back to me."

It was the old-fashioned circlet ring given by her father or mother and engraved with the words, *Jesus, Maria.* Even this innocent symbol was turned against her by her judges.

It was no wonder that in that great assembly some hearts less hardened, less jaundiced than the rest, were moved to pity for the gallant Maid in her helpless position. One of her judges, Nicolas de Houppeville, even protested that it was not lawful for Cauchon, Bishop of Beauvais, to sit as chief judge, since he was a Burgundian, and therefore incapable of taking an unprejudiced view. For this protest he was thrown into prison.

A lawyer of Rouen, Jean de Lohier, declared that the trial was not valid on certain technical grounds, and especially because she, a simple girl, was not allowed counsel, "for see how they are going on!" he said. "They will catch her in her words, as when she says 'I know for certain that

I touched the Apparition.' If she had said 'so it seemed to me,' I think no man could condemn her."

For this upright declaration, Lohier was presently forced to flee from France for his life.

The reporter, Manchon, also makes a statement that shows his indignant pity for the Maid under an unjust judge.

"Monseigneur of Beauvais would have everything written *as pleased him,* and when there was anything that displeased him, he forbad the secretaries to report it as being of no importance to the trial."

Even the evidence of the priest, Massieu, the Sheriff's officer and practically her gaoler, is to the same effect. He met an English clerk who was one of the followers of the Bishop of Winchester, and who asked him, "What do you think of her answers? Will she be burnt? What will happen?"

"Up to this time," says the cautious Massieu, "I have heard nothing from her that was not honourable and good. She seems to me a good woman, but how it will all end God only knows."

Once, indeed, the whole court, in its startled silence, seemed to show sympathy with the Maid.

She had said again and again that, had it not been for the grace of God, she would not have known how to act, when one of her judges asked, probably with a sneer, "How do you know you are in the grace of God?"

An Augustinian monk, who formed one of the court, interposed pityingly, "That is a great matter to answer. Perhaps the accused is not bound to answer upon it."

At once the bullying voice of the Bishop silenced him. "You would have done better to be quiet!"

A heated discussion followed as to the propriety of the question, which was at length again put to Jeanne.

"Speak, Jeanne; do you know yourself to be in the grace of God?"

Most pathetically rang out the piteous voice of the Maid:

"If I am not, God bring me to it! If I am, God keep me in it! I should be of all women most miserable if I knew myself to be out of the love and favour of God."

The silence that followed was broken by the words of an archdeacon, more courageous than the rest:

"Jeanne, thou hast answered well!"

When the trial was resumed after this long and embarrassed pause, the questioner dealt with quite other matters.

XVI
THE EXAMINATION IN THE PRISON
March–May 1431

Aie bon courage, prends ton martyre en gré;
tu seras bientôt délivrée, et tu viendras finalement
au royaumedu Paradis
(Les Voix in the prison)

FOR six days the public examination had dragged along its weary course. At the end of that time several significant changes had occurred in the procedure of the trial. Of the sixty-eight judges who presided on the second day, twenty-four had managed on some excuse or other to slip away altogether, as though ashamed of the part they had come to play.

In Rouen itself a change was clearly coming over public opinion. The lawyer Lohier, whom we have already seen objecting to the legality of the trial, had now openly declared that he would have nothing more to do with it. The priest, Massieu, who, as warder of the Maid, had had occasion to watch her most closely, was heard again to declare his belief in her innocence.

Moreover, from the crowd who stood by as listeners to the evidence, there had more than once risen a cry of "Well said!" and even an English knight, belonging to the most prejudiced party of all, had called out on one occasion, after a more than usually spirited reply, "Why was this brave Maid not an Englishwoman?"

It really seemed as though public opinion, which had formerly clamoured for Jeanne to be burnt as a witch, was now veering round to her side so completely as to make her condemnation a matter of difficulty if not of impossibility.

This, to the minds of the Burgundian Bishop and his English friends, was an intolerable position; and forthwith, after much consultation, the public examination was closed.

A week later, a small committee was appointed to examine her, three or four of them at a time, in prison.

Here conditions were very much harder for the Maid. She no longer had a breath of fresh air, a glance at the spring sunshine as she crossed the courtyard. No crowd of spectators sustained her with an ever-increasing sympathy. If one of her judges seemed to be favourably inclined to her, it was not difficult to exclude him for the future.

It is no wonder then that for the first time we find the splendid nerves of the Maid beginning to show signs of strain. The first symptom of this was curious enough. Her interlocutors took the opportunity to press her very hard again upon the subject of the sign she had given to the King on her first appearance at Chinon.

She had already refused several times to discuss this, saying indeed that "she would rather have her head cut off than reveal the divine communication to her sovereign."

Now, however, when hard pressed, she suddenly let loose a flood of information, vague, mystifying, unsatisfactory to a degree. Those who have most closely studied her character and history explain the matter thus. She had been badgered beyond endurance by those who insisted that there was a sign—a matter about which she had refused to give any information whatever. Weary, bored, and possibly inspired by an impulse almost of girlish mischief, a wish to mislead and mystify these learned men, a wish also to end the matter by inventing something, anything, to satisfy them, she composed a long tale

of wonder, which, while really telling them nothing definite, was full of mysterious details. If it did not satisfy
them, let them try some other line. *Passez-outre!*

Or it may have been indeed the feverish excitement of
an over-strained mind that thus drew Jeanne away from
her usually calm and accurate rejoinders.

In what followed we lose also the note of hopefulness
that had been so marked at the beginning of the trial.

They asked her if her Voices had spoken to her of late
in her cell; and she answered gravely:

"Yes; they say to me, 'Have good courage; take thy
martyrdom cheerfully; thou shalt soon be delivered and
thou shalt come at last to the kingdom of Paradise.'"

She added, sadly, that she knew not whether she had
still more to suffer, but she waited for the will of her Lord.

Her judges then began a long and tedious examination,
directed to prove that she refused to submit to the
Church on the question regarding the nature of her
Voices. This was the most trying part of all to Jeanne,
whose faith was that of a simple child, who could be
caught tripping over and over again by hostile clerics,
learned in theology; and who knew, moreover, that the
Church, in this sense, signified the English and
Burgundian ecclesiastics.

At first, when the words "Submission to the Church"
were mentioned, she brightened up and said boldly that
"she ought to be allowed to go to church."

They asked her if she did not think it unbecoming for
her to hear Mass in a boy's dress, to which she replied
that she would wear a woman's dress on that occasion, if
they would promise to let her go to church.

Half teasing, they promised it, insisting on the change of
attire, however, with such force and meaning that Jeanne
drew back. She would not give up her tight-fitting boy's
dress altogether.

"Let me have a long skirt without a train and go to Mass.
On returning I will wear my boy's suit."

They refused, upon which she declared she would not

give up her present garb at all; and the matter dropped for the time.

The whole question of the dress was dwelt on and much exaggerated by her judges. The real explanation of the fact seems to be that Jeanne clung to her boy's dress for two reasons.

It had been indispensable during her rough life in the camp, and even more so during those first months in prison, when she was exposed to the rude horse-play and unseemly jokes of the English archers. It had, moreover, as we have already noted, become to her the outward symbol of her Call and her Work; at the desire of the King alone had she reluctantly laid it by for a time, and she implied in one of her answers that only at his command would she relinquish it now. The dress they had tried to force upon her in prison was the short frock of a peasant girl. Humble as she was, she had no mind to degrade her high calling by unseemly attire. She had worn the robe of a noble lady at the Court, and she now demanded at least the long dress of a citizen's daughter in which to go to church. As this was denied her, she would keep to her boy's garb.

But a few days later the shadow had darkened in that gloomy cell, and for the first time she had a premonition of the end. They had urged her again to say if she would submit to the judgment of the Church; and she had answered, with troubled looks, "I submit myself to Our Lord and Our Lady and all the Blessed Saints in Paradise; Our Lord and the Church are one. Why do you make a difficulty as if it were not?"

They explained that they referred to the Church Militant on Earth; and she said emphatically, "I came to the King of France on the part of God and the Church Triumphant above, and to that Church I submit all my good deeds and all that I have done or shall do."

Poor little Maid! She was no heretic, though they twisted her simple speech into something resembling heresy; but she knew that for her at that moment, the

Church below meant the Bishop of Beauvais and his implacable friends, and to their judgment she would not submit her Divine Voices, her call from above. She knew, moreover, as she watched their grim faces kindle with satisfaction at her refusal, that the net was being drawn closer and closer round her girlish limbs; and when they harped again on the subject of her dress, it was with anxious eyes and troubled face that she, foreseeing shame and possible dishonour, said with trembling earnestness:

"I will not put on this woman's dress yet—not until it shall please God. But if I am brought to death, and I must be unclothed to die, I beg of you, my lords of the Church, that you will have the charity to allow me a woman's long shift, and a kerchief for my head." Then she steadies her faltering voice and adds firmly, "For I would rather die than revoke what God has caused me to do; but I believe firmly that He will never let me be brought so low, and that I shall have His help, and by a miracle."

"Why do you ask for a woman's shift if you wear man's dress by command of God?" they asked curiously; but she only repeated her pitiful little request.

"It is enough that it should be long."

Surely even those hard hearts must have been touched with pity for the helpless girl, with the fire and the stake in view, whose chief dread is of the rude gaze of the soldiery upon her shrinking form, stripped of the garb that had been her protection until now.

In the afternoon of that day, she made her pathetic appeal to be judged by the Pope himself. Half jeering, they had asked her if she would feel bound to speak more fully before the Holy Father than she had done before "my lord of Beauvais."

She leaped at the suggestion. "I demand to be taken before him! Before *him* I will answer all that I ought to."

This alone was enough to prove her loyalty to the Church, but she was not thus to escape the toils that had been spread so carefully for her. They hastily turned to another subject and asked if it were true that her standard had been carried into the cathedral at Rheims when those of the other captains had remained outside. Her answer rings out with the brave spirit of old:

"It had been through the labour and the pain! Reason good that it should have the honour!"

On March 17th, the eve of Passion Sunday, the long examination came to an end. For the next few days a group of learned doctors busied themselves in drawing up twelve articles containing the chief points of indictment against the Maid, and then in considering them one by one. They came to the conclusion that "the Visions and Voices were either 'human inventions' or the work of devils; that Jeanne's evidence was a tissue of lies; that she was blasphemous towards God and impious towards her parents; schismatic as regarded the Church, and so forth."[1] And meantime this poor little "heretic" was pleading that she might be allowed to hear Mass on Palm Sunday, and be allowed to approach the sacraments of Confession and Holy Communion at Easter.

The Bishop and four others had come to her cell very early that Palm Sunday morning, and they insisted that she must wear the peasant's dress if she were allowed this; but by this time, to the Maid's overstrained and weary mind, the boy's garb had become an absolutely sacred symbol of her loyalty to God and His Saints; to give this up was to relinquish her case and to disobey her Master.

"My Voices do not advise me to do it; I cannot do it yet," she said.

They began to entreat her with apparent kindness and good-will, to reconsider her decision.

"If it depended on me, it would soon be done," she replied sadly.

"Will you consult your Voices as to whether you may change it, so as to have your Easter Communion?" urged the Bishop.

---

[1]Andrew Lang, *The Maid of France.*

"I cannot change it—not even to receive my Saviour!" she said. "Let me hear Mass to-day as I am. My dress is no burden on my soul—to wear it is not against the Church."

But they thought otherwise. By this time even to them the whole question of the garments worn by Jeanne had assumed abnormal proportions. To relinquish her boy's dress was to "submit to the Church," and her refusal was but another addition, in their eyes, to her list of crimes.

XVII
The "Abjuration" of Jeanne
May 1431

Je me soumettra
(The words of Jeanne at her Abjuration)

THE consideration of the Twelve Articles by which the Maid had offended gave Cauchon, Bishop of Beauvais, more trouble than he had expected. The old Archbishop of Avranches, for example, a man learned in theology, declared that, according to the doctrines of St. Thomas of Aquin, the greatest authority in the Church, Jeanne had said nothing amiss. Others were by no means emphatic in giving their opinion against her, but expressed their willingness to abide by the decision of the University of Paris. This decision was couched in unmistakable terms. "Jeanne had been delivered over to Satan" and must be condemned as a heretic.

Meantime the Maid had fallen ill. The marvel is that she had retained her health so long, seeing that for months she had lain fettered in a dark, unwholesome cell, from which she had only emerged for a week to be questioned and harassed before the Court. Her most sympathetic historian[1] says that her heart began to fail her on that Palm Sunday when they would not let her go to church as she had begged.

-----

[1]Michelet.

The *beau jour de Pâques fleuries* would be especially dear to the country girl, who had lived among the trees green with spring buds, who loved the fresh air, and who had doubtless in bygone days often helped to gather the sprigs of flowering willow, which were blessed and distributed to the faithful on that day. But now it was passed by her in that gloomy cell, *au fond de la tour,* where she lay watching the fast-closed door with longing, pitiful gaze.

No wonder she broke down in health, and that when she was brought forth on the Tuesday in Holy Week to the great hall of the castle, she was found languid, feverish, dispirited, yet holding quite firmly to her convictions.

Her judges talked to her gently and kindly. They did not want to be revenged on her, not even to punish her, but merely to put her in the way of truth and safety. They would instruct her and admonish her for her good.

The Maid's eyes were keen enough in spite of languor and sickness. She glanced from one face to the other; she noted the hostile looks, the uneasy smile, the pretence of friendliness; and she replied quite gently but very steadily. "In that you admonish me for my good, I thank you; as to the advice you offer me, I have no intention of departing from the counsel of my Lord."

As usual they returned to the charge of her wearing man's dress, and insisted that she should give this up. She answered wearily that "it was not for her to say when she would do that."

They reminded her again that Easter was near, and that she would not be allowed to hear Mass in her present attire. With a flash of the old spirit she replied, "Oh, well, Our Lord can quite well cause me to hear it without you."

After two days of this examination, the Maid lay in her gloomy cell, silent save for the rough rude talk of the men-at-arms, till Easter Eve. During that time several of her judges managed to slip away; they were not anxious to see the miserable business to its close; but on the Saturday, when those who remained visited the cell they found the girl had regained something of her former cheerfulness.

"*Associant les souffrances à celles du Christ, elle s'était relevée,*" says Michelet; and we can well see how that long Good Friday spent in quiet meditation may have brought new strength and steadfastness to the girl who was following so closely in her Master's steps.

When they once more asked her if she would submit to the Church, she replied with quiet dignity, "Yes, if it does not command me to do anything impossible to me." In that case she said again and again she would submit to no man but only to her Lord.

Easter came, and with it a present of a carp to the young prisoner from Monseigneur de Beauvais, after eating which Jeanne became so alarmingly ill that the general opinion of the day was that it had been poisoned. This is quite unlikely, for her death in prison would have frustrated all his intentions, and, as a matter of fact, doctors were sent to her cell, and every effort made to recover her. Yet still we see her chained to that bed of sickness, and left to the haphazard nursing of the soldiers who guarded her, though she was so ill that she herself thought she would die.

"I think I am in great danger of death," she said pitifully to her judges when they visited her, "and I implore you that I may confess myself and receive Holy Communion and be buried in holy ground."

"If you would have the Sacraments you must submit to Holy Church."

"I cannot say anything more about that," she said wearily.

For a fortnight they left her alone. Then finding her slightly better in health, they determined to try and frighten her into submission. On May 9th they brought her into a grim chamber where lay the instruments of torture, racks and screws, and showed her the executioners ready for their terrible task.

She may have blanched at the sight, but indignation roused her to a spirited reply.

"Truly if you tore me limb from limb, till my soul is forced from my body, I will say no other thing than I have said. And if I do, I will always declare that you dragged it from me by force."

So the judge "seeing the manner of her replies, and her obdurate mind, and fearing that the agony of torture would not do her any good, postponed it till they had further counsel."

A week later came the reply of the Council of the University of Paris, already referred to, which condemned her as an "obstinate heretic."

For one terrible week of uncertainty they left the Maid alone in her cell, while they debated upon what should next be done to her. The declaration of the University had ended thus:

"If the aforesaid woman, charitably exhorted by competent judges, does not return spontaneously to the Catholic faith, publicly abjure her errors, and give full satisfaction to her judges, she is hereby given up to the secular judge to receive the reward of her deeds."

By this time her unwilling judges had been brought back again to their post. They knew that the sentence just read implied the terrible death at the stake, yet some there were who would hasten on to that end without further delay. Others, more merciful, recommended that Jeanne should once more be "charitably exhorted," and accordingly she was again brought into the Hall and made to listen to the Twelve Articles of Accusation.

She heard in silence, and when asked what she had to say for herself, silence was still her answer. She might well have been overwhelmed by the terrible indictment into which learned divines had twisted her simple answers, her sincere words. She guessed, too, what was the end in sight, as is seen in the words which at length fell with pitiful expression from her trembling lips.

"If I were at judgment; if I saw the fire kindled and the faggots ablaze, and the executioner ready to stir the fire; and if I were in the fire, I would say no more, and till death I will maintain what I have said is the truth."

Responsio Johannæ superba—the "proud reply of

Jeanne"—is the comment made in the margin of his manuscript by the scribe who took down her words, and he
adds:

"And immediately the promoter and she refusing to say
more, the cause was concluded."

One more attempt to shake her resolution was made,
and the scene in which it occurs is the darkest of Jeanne's
young life. To understand its grim purport we must
remember, first, that it was not at all to the mind of
Cauchon that his victim should go to the stake still firm in
her innocence, unmoved in her declaration that her
Voices were of God. It has been well said by one of her
biographers that "the popular mind has a tendency to
embrace beliefs maintained to the death; and if Jeanne
could so maintain the verity of her revelations, some of
which none could deny had been gloriously fulfilled,
dead, she would have a following such as in her day of
honour she had never numbered."[1] Hence it was necessary that by hook or by crook she should be frightened
into some sort of submission and abjuration.

But, on the other hand, the English party, under the
nominal direction of the Bishop of Winchester and the
Earl of Warwick, were equally determined that no such
abjuration should save Jeanne's life. By the law of the
Church, such a submission would admit the prisoner to
"penitence," generally lifelong, within the ecclesiastical
prisons. The English would not run the risk of any such
thing. A popular rising in favour of the Maid, a turn in the
popular opinion even, would set her free, and all the trouble would begin over again.

So, by some means or another, Jeanne must abjure and
yet must be burnt as a heretic; and these two facts must
be borne in mind in surveying the few remaining scenes of
her life.

Jeanne had had a restless, dispiriting night after the
French trial had ended, and the soft May sunshine, as it fil-

---

[1]Parr, *Life and Death of Jeanne d' Arc.*

tered in through the bars of her dungeon window, found her weary, nervous, ill at ease. Her Voices had ceased of late—that was her chief source of trouble, though they had for some time past been so vague as to be almost useless to her. Their promise, made long weeks ago, that within three months there would be aid for her, and a great victory, seemed quite unfulfilled. The end of May was fast approaching, and with it the period of three months would be over. For perhaps the first time she knew the bitter misery of doubt. Had she, after all, been mistaken? Had all her courage, her constancy, been in vain?

To her, in those early morning hours, came one of her more kindly judges, Jean Beaupère, who told her that on this very day she would be taken to the scaffold to be preached to before the people. "Now, if you are a good Christian, you will say there, on the scaffold, that all your words and deeds you will submit to the ordinances of holy Mother Church, and especially of your ecclesiastical judges."

Whether she made any reply is not clear, but presently, as though in a dream, she found herself being drawn in a car through shouting throngs of people who pressed upon her, some with savage threats, many with looks of pity, as she glanced about her with eyes dazed by the bright spring sunshine. It was three months since she had breathed the fresh air of the outside world, three months of almost incessant harass. Her young limbs, stiff with the pressure of heavy fetters, stretched themselves gladly, her young heart was fired with hope. What girl of nineteen, deserted by her friends, alternately coaxed and bullied by learned men, men who represented the Church she had always loved, could have stood out longer against their urgent representations?

A cold shadow fell upon her soul as she saw with a shudder, in the midst of the market-place, a high scaffold with a stake upon it and faggots ready for the burning. Only the victim was wanting, and there were those in that crowd who did not hesitate to draw her attention to the grim spectacle with mocking cries as the car in which she sat rattled past over the cobble stones of the square.

In the great churchyard of St. Ouen two platforms had been erected, on one of which sat Cardinal Beaufort, Bishop of Winchester, Cauchon, Bishop of Beauvais, and about forty other judges. On the other platform stood a pulpit for the preacher, and a place for Jeanne, who stood there in her worn, dark suit, with Massieu close beside her. The sermon was preached by Guillaume Erard, unwillingly enough, it was true, though it is a fact that, as he warmed to his task, he used terms of reproach and shame that were more than unnecessary. To these Jeanne listened in silence. Perhaps she scarcely heard him; perhaps her thoughts were busy with the distant line of country she could see beyond the walls, or with that dark scaffold in the market-place. Suddenly, however, her attention was arrested. The preacher had raised his voice, was pointing to her, and in loud tones was crying out: "It is to *thee,* Jeanne, I speak, and I tell thee thy King is a heretic and a schismatic!"

The words instantly roused all the loyalty of the Maid, and her voice rang out distinct and clear:

"Say of me what you like, but let the King be! By my faith I swear upon my life that my King is the most noble Christian of all Christians, that he is not what you say."

"Make her hold her peace," cried Cauchon and the outraged preacher in one breath; and so the "sermon" proceeded to the bitter end. When he had finished, the Maid's voice once more rang out, though now more subdued in tone.

"I will answer you. I have told them that all the works that I have done or said may be sent to Rome, to the Holy Father, to whom, but to God first, I refer in all."

"That is not enough. The Pope is too far off, and every Bishop is judge in his own diocese," she was told.

Again and again they urged her, and three times "definitely admonished her that she should submit to Holy

Church," and finally the Bishop of Beauvais began to read aloud the sentence passed upon her as a heretic.

In the official records we find this one brief, pregnant note inserted by Manchon the scribe:

"At the end of the sentence, Jeanne fearing the fire, said she would obey the Church."

What actually happened seems to have been as follows. After her declaration that she would submit to the Pope and the refusal of her judges to accept this, two forms of "abjuration," one long and formal, the other very brief, were brought forward, and the latter was handed to Massieu by Erard, who said at the same time to Jeanne, "Jeanne, thou wilt abjure and sign that schedule."

"But I do not know what it means to 'abjure,'" cried the Maid, bewildered by the loud voices, the angry faces, the bullying words.

Massieu did his best to help her. "To abjure means, Jeanne, that if ever you go contrary to any of the points written in this document, you will be burnt." He added privately, hoping to save her, "I advise you therefore to appeal to the Catholic Church as to whether you ought to sign it."

She caught at this, crying out, "I appeal to the Catholic Church," but Erard only raged back at her, "Thou shalt sign it at once or be burnt!"

"But I cannot write!" she wailed, and cast despairing eyes over the crowd below, from which, from time to time, cries of pity and encouragement ascended.

"Save yourself, Jeanne, why should you die?"

"Sign! Sign!"

Once indeed she flung them back her answer, her declaration of innocence.

"All that I have done, all that I do is well done, and I have done well to do it!"

But there was, perhaps, beneath the brave words a note of despairing doubt.

Still they pressed, urged, bullied her; and at length the Bishop of Beauvais began slowly to read the sentence of condemnation. Half-way through, Erard was busy again at Jeanne's ear.

"Thou *must* abjure! If thou wilt do what thou art coun-selled to do thou shalt be released from prison."

She wavered, while a mingled shout of pity and of wrath as they saw the chance of their prey escaping rose from the crowd below.

"*I will submit.*"

The piteous cry must have rung out in the momentary silence that followed. The Bishop stopped immediately, much to the wrath of an Englishman, chaplain to the Cardinal, who muttered, "Monseigneur favours the woman."

Cauchon might well reply angrily, "There is no favour-ing in such a case!" He knew the inevitable end.

Meantime Massieu read aloud to Jeanne the formula of recantation in which she was made to say that "she had lyingly feigned to have had revelations and apparitions from God, by the angels, and St. Margaret and St. Catherine: that she had worn an immodest dress against nature . . . that she had grievously erred in the faith."

Well might a bystander note that the Maid openly smiled as she heard the high-sounding words—smiled, possibly, in self-scorn, but also at the absurdity of such admissions.

Even then they tricked her, for at once she was given to sign a much longer paper of recantation, and at that she took alarm, saying, "Let this be seen by the Clergy and by the Church in whose hands I ought to be put; and if they counsel me to sign it, I will obey!"

But it was too late for this; probably Erard threatened her with "Sign, or burn!" upon which she hastily "made a cross with the pen which the witness handed to her."

As a matter of fact, though this is the report of Massieu, she made a round O at the foot of the shorter paper, and it is still a matter of conjecture how the signature *Jehanne*, scrawled at the end of the longer document, was obtained.

A scene of confusion followed. The English soldiers in the crowd began to throw stones at the judges in their wrath at what they considered deliverance for Jeanne. Scarce could the Bishop's voice be heard as he hastily read a sentence releasing her from excommunication and ending thus: "But since you have sinned against God and the Church we condemn you, in our grace and moderation, to pass the rest of your days in prison, on the bread of sorrow and the water of anguish, there to weep and lament your sins, and commit no more for the future."

A pause of uncertainty followed. Had Jeanne really hoped for release her heart must have sunk at Cauchon's words, but she seems rather to have heard the sentence with relief. While the Bishops hastily conferred as to what they should do with her next, while one of her false friends was pretending to congratulate her with oily words, "Jeanne, you have done a good day's work, you have saved your soul," she was trembling with eagerness for the fulfilment of the decree.

"Men of the Church," she cried, with sharp anxiety in her voice, "lead me to your prison. Let me be no longer in the hands of the English!"

Alas! it was not to be so. The representatives of English prejudice and French injustice had already agreed that she should not thus escape. "Take her back whence you brought her," commanded Cauchon, and with that the Maid knew that her abjuration had been made in vain.

Broken in spirit, she was led back to that dismal cell, to the fetters, to the odious company of her gaolers; and when some of her judges visited her that afternoon, bringing with them a peasant maiden's dress, she meekly accepted it.

Three dreadful days followed that sad Thursday; and then news was brought to Cauchon that she had returned to her boy's garb. The news was by no means unexpected. The change of attire had been the outward sign of her submission, and the English, either with or without his help, had their ways and means of securing a "relapse." When some of her judges hastened to the prison to find out the truth, the men-at-arms drove them back, refusing entrance. They had not completely worked their will upon the Maid.

When at length Cauchon and some others obtained entrance to the dungeon, they found her in boy's attire, "her face wet with tears, disfigured, and outraged." Asked why she had gone back to this, she said evasively "that it was more convenient to wear men's dress among men, and the promise that she should receive the Sacrament and be released from her irons had been broken."

Then the vehement voice began to quaver into a bitter wail.

"I would rather die than remain in irons. If you will release me and let me go to Mass and lie in a gentle prison, I will be good and do all that the Church desires."

Bit by bit, when the Bishop had departed, the cruel tale came out, a tale of insult and torment at the hands of the English men-at-arms, who, when she tried to rise, took away her woman's dress and left her nothing but that she had given up. But there was no more heat, no more indignation; she was full of a sadness, almost of resignation, that at once attracted the attention of her judges.

Cauchon asked her suddenly if she had heard her Voices since the day of her "Abjuration"; and she answered quietly, "Yes." They demanded to know what they had said; and she replied with the same sad resignation "that God had sent word by St. Catherine and St. Margaret how great was the pity there was in heaven that I had consented to the treason of abjuring to save my life: and that I had condemned my soul."

"Did your Voices tell you what you would do on Thursday?"

"They bade me answer the preacher boldly on that day"; and she adds with a flash of the old brave Jeanne, "I call that preacher a false man, for he said many things of me that I never did."

"Have the Voices reproached you for your abjuration?"

"They told me that it was great wickedness to confess that I had not well done. I said what I did for fear of the fire."

Finally, in answer to further questions, she made it absolutely clear that she rejected, once and for all, her forced "Abjuration."

"I have done nothing against God or the Faith, whatever you may have made me revoke: and as for what was in that document of abjuration, I did not understand it.

"If you that are my judges will put me in a safe place, I will again wear my woman's dress; for the rest I will do nothing."

It was more than enough; and the Bishops hurried away to arrange with the assessors for the final scene.

After a brief discussion, a citation was drawn up, calling upon the Maid to appear before them the next day at eight o'clock, in the Old Market-place of Rouen to undergo her sentence. This was handed to Massieu to be given to her on the morning of the day of execution.

The grim story goes on to say that, as the Bishop of Beauvais emerged from the chapel after these arrangements had been made, the Earl of Warwick hastened to meet him and to learn the latest news. Whereupon the Bishop, greeting him with much satisfaction, was heard to say, "Make good cheer! The thing is done!"

XVIII

IN ROUEN MARKET-PLACE
May 30, 1431

Oui, mes Voix étaient de Dieu,
mes Voix ne m'ont pas trompée!
(Jeanne's words on the scaffold)

VERY early on the morning of the 30th May a certain Friar Martin entered the girl's cell with the fatal message. Massieu, as we know, was to have delivered it; perhaps his heart, ever tender toward his young charge, failed him at the last.

The Maid, roughly awakened by the friar's entrance, heard what he had to say, and forthwith broke down in a most natural outburst of grief. She loved her life as much as most girls of nineteen; what marvel is it that on this bright May morning she had no mind to die? She wept sorely, crying out:

"Alas, am I to be so horribly and cruelly treated? Alas, that my body, whole and entire, which has ever been kept in purity, should to-day be consumed and burnt to ashes! Ah, I would far rather have my head cut off, seven times over, than be thus burnt! Had I been in the prison of the Church to which I submitted myself, and guarded by the Clergy instead of by mine enemies, it would not have fallen out so unhappily for me. I appeal to God, the great judge, for the evils and injustice done me."

The friar strove, charitably enough, to soothe her and prepare her for her end, and presently a great calm of sadness fell upon her, and "in most humble and contrite fashion" she received at length the Sacraments for which she had hungered and thirsted so long.

Even at that supreme moment they could not leave her in peace. One of the "praying men" who was present, declares that, at the moment of the administration of the Host, the friar asked her, "Do you believe that this is the Body of Christ?" To which she replied, "Yes, and He alone can deliver me; I pray you to administer."

"Do you believe as fully in your Voices?" he persisted; and she answered, "I believe in God, but not in my Voices, for they have deceived me."

For the moment it seemed indeed as though the steadfast spring of hope and faith had run dry, for she admitted the same to Cauchon, when that prelate hurried, with indecent haste, to see her in her forlorn condition.

"So, Jeanne, you see now your Voices have not delivered you and that they have deceived you. Tell us now the truth."

To which she answered very sadly, "Yes, I see they have

indeed deceived me." Then with a flash of her old fiery spirit, she turns upon him with:

"Bishop, 'tis through you I die! For this I summon you before God!"

Perhaps one of those who lingered after the Bishop had departed looked with some kindness on the poor child, for she said to him, "Ah, sir, where shall I be to-night?"

He had condemned her but lately as an obstinate heretic, but now he answered, not as a prejudiced judge, but as a man in whose heart charity was not yet dead:

"Have you not good faith in your Lord?"

To which she replied fervently, "Ah yes, God helping me, I shall be in Paradise."

They arrayed her in the long white shift of the penitent, and placed upon her head a mitre, inscribed with the words, "Heretic, Relapsed, Apostate, Idolater," and thus they led her out to die. Massieu and the friar who had been with her in the prison sat beside her in the car, drawn by four horses, that was to take her to the Market-place.

She wept, like the child she was, as she saw the gay world of Rouen glittering in the bright May sunshine, the crowds that thronged around the car, the tower of the cathedral in the distance. "Rouen, Rouen, is it here I must die?" they heard her sob; and again, as the car creaked forward on its way, "Rouen, Rouen, I fear that you shall yet suffer because of this!"

They could not even let her die in peace. She was made to mount one of three scaffolds, on the second of which stood her judges, and on the third a mass of plaster, on which stood the faggots and the stake. There, in full sight of the hostile crowd, was fastened a great placard recounting the reasons for her condemnation; and there she was made to stand and listen to another sermon full of swelling words and harsh invective.

Those who stood nearest to her—probably Massieu and the friar—bear witness that the Maid paid no attention to all this, but "knelt on the platform, showing great

signs and appearance of contrition, so that all those who
looked upon her wept. She called on her knees upon the
Blessed Trinity, the blessed and glorious Virgin Mary, and
all the blessed Saints of Paradise. She begged right
humbly also the forgiveness of all sorts and conditions of
men, both of her own party and of her enemies; asking
them for their prayers, forgiving them for the evil they
had done her."

Even the hard-hearted Bishops of Winchester and
Beauvais wept; the waiting crowd shed "hot tears" at the
pitiful sight; but some of the brutal English soldiers cried
out in impatience, "Priests, do you want to make us dine
here?"

"Do your duty!" said Cauchon to the executioner, and
forthwith the Maid was led to the third scaffold and told
to mount to the stake. Was it then or earlier that the loud,
pitiful cry rang over the upturned heads below?

"St. Michael! St. Michael! St. Michael, help!"

Before the executioner bound her to the stake, Jeanne
asked earnestly for a cross. Maître Massieu asked the
Clerk of the Church of St. Saviour, close by, to fetch the
Church Cross, and, meantime, an English soldier, evidently much touched at sight of her suffering, broke his *bâton*
and fastened the two pieces together cross-wise. This she
received with tears of joy and put at once into her breast.
When the Church Cross was brought, says Massieu, "she
embraced it closely and long, and kept it till she was fastened to the stake."

Even then he held it up close before her that her dying
eyes might rest upon the figure of her Crucified Lord; till
she, ever mindful of others, bade him withdraw a little lest
the fire should catch his robes.

The flames shot up, the thick black smoke hid that
white figure, that sweet upturned face from the watching
crowd below.

Suddenly from the midst of the awful silence her voice
rang out, sweet and clear as in the old days when storm-
ing a redoubt or leading a forlorn hope:

"My Voices were of God! They have not deceived me!"
Once again they heard her speak.
"Jesus! Jesus!"
And with that cry of perfect recognition, of purest joy, the soul of the White Maid of France passed to the gates of Paradise.

They found the brave heart untouched by the fire, but this, together with her ashes, was thrown into the Seine, "for the English feared that some might believe she had escaped."

From the moment of her martyrdom the tide of popular opinion began to turn; and one, Maître Tressart, lamented to a fellow-citizen as they left the spot:

"We are all lost; we have burnt a Saint!"

Nearly five hundred years later, the verdict of the Catholic Church, speaking by the lips of Pope Pius X, ratified those very words; for in the year 1909, in St. Peter's at Rome, the Maid of France was declared to be one of that noble company whom for all generations men shall call Blessed.

XIX

IN AFTER-DAYS
1432–1909

*Jeanne brille comme un nouveau astre destiné être
la gloire non seulement de la France,
mais de l' Eglise Universelle.*
(Declaration of Pius X)

LET us take a brief glance at the condition of affairs in France while the weary months of the Maid's trial were dragging along.

At the moment the English had gained possession of the Maid, things were going very badly with them and with their Burgundian allies. We have seen how Burgundy had failed to take Compiègne. Another town of that district was also able to defy him, and when Saintrailles, a French captain, offered him battle in the open field, he felt it wise to refuse.

With the English, things were going still worse. Instead of taking fresh towns, one city after another, even those in the neighbourhood of Anglo-Burgundian Paris, expelled the English and went over to the side of Charles.

It was as though the spirit of the Maid were still at work, though her girlish body lay fast fettered in her cell.

To improve the parlous position of the English, the Bishop of Winchester had two plans afoot. By the trial of Jeanne d'Arc he hoped utterly to discredit the cause of the French King by showing that he had been under the influence all the time of witchcraft.

By the coronation of the child Henry, "King of France and England," he hoped to strengthen the cause of England by leaving no doubt in the mind of disaffected France as to who was their lawful and anointed sovereign.

How far the first plan succeeded we have seen enough to guess. That even the English soldiers were impressed by the innocence of Jeanne is clear; that an immense reaction in her favour took place in the minds of the French all over the land is clearer still. Not only in Rouen was the terrifying rumour whispered, "We are lost; we have burnt a Saint."

Possibly the whole position might have been worked round in favour of England now, had there been presented to France a hero-king, a prince of chivalry, such as the Black Prince of former days, or the Henry of Agincourt.

But there was nothing whatever to stir the sentiment of the nation in the little pale-faced Henry VI, timid, nervous, brow-beaten by my Lord of Warwick, trembling before Monseigneur of Winchester.

When the Coronation took place at Paris in the December before the trial of the Maid, not a single Frenchman of note was present. Even the Bishop of Paris was not asked to officiate in his own cathedral of Notre Dame, but the ceremony was carried out by the English

Cardinal, and, according to English usage, "to the great scandal of the cathedral chapter." At the Coronation banquet the great French merchants were "left to stand in the mud at the palace gate."

This was not the way to make a king popular among a people already sighing for a sovereign of their own race. After this *fiasco* of a ceremony, curiously enough, the little King was brought back from Paris to London by way of Rouen, where he was lodged for a brief period in the Castle, not far from where Jeanne was lying in her dungeon.

We remember that she "said she had no wish to see him," but one can but conjecture with interest what would have been the character of an interview between the bravest of Maids and the most faint-hearted of boys.

The next step in the downfall of English power in France was the breaking of the Burgundian alliance. The bluff Duke was not pleased to find himself on the losing side; the many blunders of the English captains in the battlefield had bred contempt in his mind for his allies; the secret marriage of the Duke of Bedford, a man of fifty, with a young girl of seventeen, daughter of one of the Duke's vassals, did not draw the links closer, but since Burgundy's permission had not been asked, almost led to an open rupture. Neither would meet the other or give way to the other.

Meantime the House of Anjou, to which family belonged the wife of the true King of France, was rallying to the help of Charles. René, the "good duke," brother-in-law of the King, was intent on winning the friendship of Burgundy; if that were gained the spectacle of a united France was within sight. For Paris, groaning under the rule of Cauchon and his Bishops, was more than willing to expel them and the English at one blow; and Normandy, headquarters of the Anglo-French party, was weary of a war that was working her destruction, and more than ready to make peace.

Then a worse blow than the tyranny of Cauchon fell

upon the capital, which was visited by a famine and a pestilence that sent Bedford in flight from its neighbourhood.

By the year 1435, three years after the death of the Maid, a Congress held at Arras strove to bring about some agreement that would end the war.

When he saw that this involved the loss of the French crown, Bedford withdrew from all negotiations, withdrew to die a few weeks later in the Castle of Rouen whence he had seen the Maid come out to meet her death.

The May of the next year saw the reconciliation between Charles and Burgundy complete, and the gates of Paris opening to receive their own legitimate sovereign.

For fifteen years more the English were to drag on a useless and hopeless war, until, driven from France in dishonour, they returned at the call of their own country, to plunge into that almost equally futile struggle known as the Wars of the Roses.

Meantime, what honour was France paying to the memory of the Maid whose wonderful skill had turned the tide of affairs and brought them, five years after her death, to this point of vantage?

In the year 1433, in an Assembly of the Three Estates (the French Parliament), held at Blois to return thanks to God "for the miraculous successes of Charles VII," not a single mention is made of Jeanne d'Arc; the honour is ascribed solely "to a little company of valiant men to whom God had given courage to undertake the cause."

Only in Metz and Compiègne the soldier-citizens mourned the memory of their brave young leader, and at Orleans, the scene of her first triumph, they kept the yearly anniversary of her martyrdom in the Church of St. Sauxon, "burning tapers, with shields of her arms attached to them, and great flambeaux of wax, while eight monks of the four mendicant orders sang masses for the repose of her soul."

But the King, that unworthy object of her unfailing loyalty and respect, never seems to have even remembered her, far less to have spoken in vindication of the cruel slanders passed upon her. She had defended him on the scaffold itself: he never troubled to say one word on her behalf when it would have cost him nothing at all.

In the year 1448 almost the only district remaining to the English was Normandy, of which the Duke of Somerset was governor. After a year's desultory fighting, the troops of Charles VII, under Jeanne's old friend and comrade Dunois, attacked and seized Rouen. In the November of that year 1449 the King took up his residence in the ancient Norman city, and there for the first time his thoughts seemed to have turned to the memory of the brave young Maid who had saved France for him at a moment when it seemed wholly lost.

Did the spirit of the White Maid haunt the walls of that gloomy castle where her King was lodged? Did her voice cry out to him from the stones of the Market-place where she had laid down her innocent life?

We cannot answer these questions; all we know is that the recreant prince issued orders that an inquiry be held concerning the circumstances of her death.

This inquiry brought to light not only Massieu, her unwilling and disapproving warder, but l'Advenu, the friar who had given her the last sacraments, and Brother Isambard, who had seen her cling to the cross while dying the death of a heretic. The report of the trial, as made by Manchon, was unearthed, and the form of the whole proceeding proved to be illegal. Cauchon, Bishop of Beauvais, had gone, ten years before, to answer for his sins before the judgment seat at which the Maid in her last hours had arraigned him; but a number of her judges were brought forward, who could only lamely plead that what they had done amiss they had done for fear of the English.

This was more than enough ground on which to base a plea for a formal revision of the whole trial; but even this, when it was gained from Rome, was obtained not by the energies of the King, but at the instance of the Maid's mother, Isambeau d'Arc and her two brothers, Pierre and Jean.

Pathetic in the extreme was the opening scene of the trial in Notre Dame, Paris, when the old and broken peasant woman, in a voice choked with tears, made her mother's plea for her famous daughter.

She had brought up her child in the fear of God, she said, and in the traditions of the Church. Her daughter had never meditated anything against the Faith; yet her enemies had accused her, and, without lawful authority, had brought her to an infamous death.

And when she broke down, and her two sons took up the plea, so many of those present joined in the petition that "at last it seemed that one great cry for justice broke from the multitude."

So the second trial was ordered, the outcome of which may be summarized in the words of one who had described her brief life-work from the time she first left home. "A beautiful life, and it would be impossible for a man to utter one word against her."

The first trial was declared to be null and void, and the judgment unjust. "The deeds of the Maid are worthy of admiration rather than of condemnation."

Forthwith two solemn processions of "Rehabilitation" were ordered, one to the churchyard of St. Ouen, the scene of the false "abjuration," the second to the market-place "where Jeanne was cruelly and horribly burnt and suffocated by fire." On the place of her execution was raised "a cross to her perpetual memory."

Thus was the innocence of the Maid set forth before the world. But this was merely an act of justice, a negative admission rather than a positive act of honour. More than four centuries were to pass before the saintly character of Jeanne and the true nature of her divine revelations were openly recognized; and then came that wonderful act of honour paid to her by the Catholic Church, known as the Beatification of Jeanne d'Arc. This ceremony took place on the 18th April 1909, in the Church of St. Peter, at Rome, where Jeanne was solemnly declared by Pope Pius X to "shine as a new star destined to be the glory not only of France, but also of the whole Church."

Like a story from some old book, that battle of long ago:
Shadows the poor French King, and the might of his
    English foe;
Shadows the charging nobles, and the archers kneeling
    a-row—
But a flame in my heart and my eyes, the Maid with her
    banner of snow!

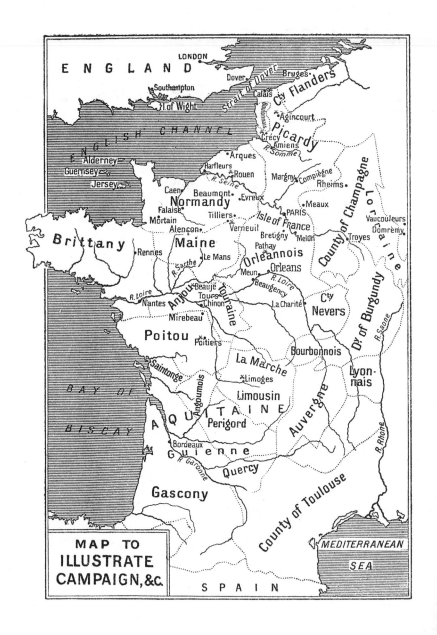

MAP TO
ILLUSTRATE
CAMPAIGN, &c.

A CATALOG OF SELECTED DOVER
BOOKS IN ALL FIELDS OF INTEREST

CONCERNING THE SPIRITUAL IN ART, Wassily Kandinsky. Pioneering work by father of abstract art. Thoughts on color theory, nature of art. Analysis of earlier masters. 12 illustrations. 80pp. of text. 5⅜ x 8½. 23411-8

ANIMALS: 1,419 Copyright-Free Illustrations of Mammals, Birds, Fish, Insects, etc., Jim Harter (ed.). Clear wood engravings present, in extremely lifelike poses, over 1,000 species of animals. One of the most extensive pictorial sourcebooks of its kind. Captions. Index. 284pp. 9 x 12. 23766-4

CELTIC ART: The Methods of Construction, George Bain. Simple geometric techniques for making Celtic interlacements, spirals, Kells-type initials, animals, humans, etc. Over 500 illustrations. 160pp. 9 x 12. (Available in U.S. only.) 22923-8

AN ATLAS OF ANATOMY FOR ARTISTS, Fritz Schider. Most thorough reference work on art anatomy in the world. Hundreds of illustrations, including selections from works by Vesalius, Leonardo, Goya, Ingres, Michelangelo, others. 593 illustrations. 192pp. 7⅛ x 10¼. 20241-0

CELTIC HAND STROKE-BY-STROKE (Irish Half-Uncial from "The Book of Kells"): An Arthur Baker Calligraphy Manual, Arthur Baker. Complete guide to creating each letter of the alphabet in distinctive Celtic manner. Covers hand position, strokes, pens, inks, paper, more. Illustrated. 48pp. 8¼ x 11. 24336-2

EASY ORIGAMI, John Montroll. Charming collection of 32 projects (hat, cup, pelican, piano, swan, many more) specially designed for the novice origami hobbyist. Clearly illustrated easy-to-follow instructions insure that even beginning papercrafters will achieve successful results. 48pp. 8¼ x 11. 27298-2

THE COMPLETE BOOK OF BIRDHOUSE CONSTRUCTION FOR WOODWORKERS, Scott D. Campbell. Detailed instructions, illustrations, tables. Also data on bird habitat and instinct patterns. Bibliography. 3 tables. 63 illustrations in 15 figures. 48pp. 5¼ x 8½. 24407-5

BLOOMINGDALE'S ILLUSTRATED 1886 CATALOG: Fashions, Dry Goods and Housewares, Bloomingdale Brothers. Famed merchants' extremely rare catalog depicting about 1,700 products: clothing, housewares, firearms, dry goods, jewelry, more. Invaluable for dating, identifying vintage items. Also, copyright-free graphics for artists, designers. Co-published with Henry Ford Museum & Greenfield Village. 160pp. 8¼ x 11. 25780-0

HISTORIC COSTUME IN PICTURES, Braun & Schneider. Over 1,450 costumed figures in clearly detailed engravings–from dawn of civilization to end of 19th century. Captions. Many folk costumes. 256pp. 8⅜ x 11¾. 23150-X

CATALOG OF DOVER BOOKS

STICKLEY CRAFTSMAN FURNITURE CATALOGS, Gustav Stickley and L. & J. G. Stickley. Beautiful, functional furniture in two authentic catalogs from 1910. 594 illustrations, including 277 photos, show settles, rockers, armchairs, reclining chairs, bookcases, desks, tables. 183pp. 6½ x 9¼. 23838-5

AMERICAN LOCOMOTIVES IN HISTORIC PHOTOGRAPHS: 1858 to 1949, Ron Ziel (ed.). A rare collection of 126 meticulously detailed official photographs, called "builder portraits," of American locomotives that majestically chronicle the rise of steam locomotive power in America. Introduction. Detailed captions. xi+ 129pp. 9 x 12. 27393-8

AMERICA'S LIGHTHOUSES: An Illustrated History, Francis Ross Holland, Jr. Delightfully written, profusely illustrated fact-filled survey of over 200 American lighthouses since 1716. History, anecdotes, technological advances, more. 240pp. 8 x 10¾. 25576-X

TOWARDS A NEW ARCHITECTURE, Le Corbusier. Pioneering manifesto by founder of "International School." Technical and aesthetic theories, views of industry, economics, relation of form to function, "mass-production split" and much more. Profusely illustrated. 320pp. 6⅛ x 9¼. (Available in U.S. only.) 25023-7

HOW THE OTHER HALF LIVES, Jacob Riis. Famous journalistic record, exposing poverty and degradation of New York slums around 1900, by major social reformer. 100 striking and influential photographs. 233pp. 10 x 7⅞. 22012-5

FRUIT KEY AND TWIG KEY TO TREES AND SHRUBS, William M. Harlow. One of the handiest and most widely used identification aids. Fruit key covers 120 deciduous and evergreen species; twig key 160 deciduous species. Easily used. Over 300 photographs. 126pp. 5⅜ x 8½. 20511-8

COMMON BIRD SONGS, Dr. Donald J. Borror. Songs of 60 most common U.S. birds: robins, sparrows, cardinals, bluejays, finches, more–arranged in order of increasing complexity. Up to 9 variations of songs of each species. Cassette and manual 99911-4

ORCHIDS AS HOUSE PLANTS, Rebecca Tyson Northen. Grow cattleyas and many other kinds of orchids–in a window, in a case, or under artificial light. 63 illustrations. 148pp. 5⅜ x 8½. 23261-1

MONSTER MAZES, Dave Phillips. Masterful mazes at four levels of difficulty. Avoid deadly perils and evil creatures to find magical treasures. Solutions for all 32 exciting illustrated puzzles. 48pp. 8¼ x 11. 26005-4

MOZART'S DON GIOVANNI (DOVER OPERA LIBRETTO SERIES), Wolfgang Amadeus Mozart. Introduced and translated by Ellen H. Bleiler. Standard Italian libretto, with complete English translation. Convenient and thoroughly portable–an ideal companion for reading along with a recording or the performance itself. Introduction. List of characters. Plot summary. 121pp. 5¼ x 8½. 24944-1

TECHNICAL MANUAL AND DICTIONARY OF CLASSICAL BALLET, Gail Grant. Defines, explains, comments on steps, movements, poses and concepts. 15-page pictorial section. Basic book for student, viewer. 127pp. 5⅜ x 8½. 21843-0

THE CLARINET AND CLARINET PLAYING, David Pino. Lively, comprehensive work features suggestions about technique, musicianship, and musical interpretation, as well as guidelines for teaching, making your own reeds, and preparing for public performance. Includes an intriguing look at clarinet history. "A godsend," *The Clarinet,* Journal of the International Clarinet Society. Appendixes. 7 illus. 320pp. 5⅜ x 8½. 40270-3

HOLLYWOOD GLAMOR PORTRAITS, John Kobal (ed.). 145 photos from 1926-49. Harlow, Gable, Bogart, Bacall; 94 stars in all. Full background on photographers, technical aspects. 160pp. 8⅜ x 11¼. 23352-9

THE ANNOTATED CASEY AT THE BAT: A Collection of Ballads about the Mighty Casey/Third, Revised Edition, Martin Gardner (ed.). Amusing sequels and parodies of one of America's best-loved poems: Casey's Revenge, Why Casey Whiffed, Casey's Sister at the Bat, others. 256pp. 5⅜ x 8½. 28598-7

THE RAVEN AND OTHER FAVORITE POEMS, Edgar Allan Poe. Over 40 of the author's most memorable poems: "The Bells," "Ulalume," "Israfel," "To Helen," "The Conqueror Worm," "Eldorado," "Annabel Lee," many more. Alphabetic lists of titles and first lines. 64pp. 5$\frac{3}{16}$ x 8¼. 26685-0

PERSONAL MEMOIRS OF U. S. GRANT, Ulysses Simpson Grant. Intelligent, deeply moving firsthand account of Civil War campaigns, considered by many the finest military memoirs ever written. Includes letters, historic photographs, maps and more. 528pp. 6⅛ x 9¼. 28587-1

ANCIENT EGYPTIAN MATERIALS AND INDUSTRIES, A. Lucas and J. Harris. Fascinating, comprehensive, thoroughly documented text describes this ancient civilization's vast resources and the processes that incorporated them in daily life, including the use of animal products, building materials, cosmetics, perfumes and incense, fibers, glazed ware, glass and its manufacture, materials used in the mummification process, and much more. 544pp. 6⅛ x 9¼. (Available in U.S. only.) 40446-3

RUSSIAN STORIES/RUSSKIE RASSKAZY: A Dual-Language Book, edited by Gleb Struve. Twelve tales by such masters as Chekhov, Tolstoy, Dostoevsky, Pushkin, others. Excellent word-for-word English translations on facing pages, plus teaching and study aids, Russian/English vocabulary, biographical/critical introductions, more. 416pp. 5⅜ x 8½. 26244-8

PHILADELPHIA THEN AND NOW: 60 Sites Photographed in the Past and Present, Kenneth Finkel and Susan Oyama. Rare photographs of City Hall, Logan Square, Independence Hall, Betsy Ross House, other landmarks juxtaposed with contemporary views. Captures changing face of historic city. Introduction. Captions. 128pp. 8¼ x 11. 25790-8

AIA ARCHITECTURAL GUIDE TO NASSAU AND SUFFOLK COUNTIES, LONG ISLAND, The American Institute of Architects, Long Island Chapter, and the Society for the Preservation of Long Island Antiquities. Comprehensive, well-researched and generously illustrated volume brings to life over three centuries of Long Island's great architectural heritage. More than 240 photographs with authoritative, extensively detailed captions. 176pp. 8¼ x 11. 26946-9

NORTH AMERICAN INDIAN LIFE: Customs and Traditions of 23 Tribes, Elsie Clews Parsons (ed.). 27 fictionalized essays by noted anthropologists examine religion, customs, government, additional facets of life among the Winnebago, Crow, Zuni, Eskimo, other tribes. 480pp. 6⅛ x 9¼. 27377-6

FRANK LLOYD WRIGHT'S DANA HOUSE, Donald Hoffmann. Pictorial essay of residential masterpiece with over 160 interior and exterior photos, plans, elevations, sketches and studies. 128pp. 9¼ x 10¾. 29120-0

THE MALE AND FEMALE FIGURE IN MOTION: 60 Classic Photographic Sequences, Eadweard Muybridge. 60 true-action photographs of men and women walking, running, climbing, bending, turning, etc., reproduced from rare 19th-century masterpiece. vi + 121pp. 9 x 12. 24745-7

1001 QUESTIONS ANSWERED ABOUT THE SEASHORE, N. J. Berrill and Jacquelyn Berrill. Queries answered about dolphins, sea snails, sponges, starfish, fishes, shore birds, many others. Covers appearance, breeding, growth, feeding, much more. 305pp. 5¼ x 8¼. 23366-9

ATTRACTING BIRDS TO YOUR YARD, William J. Weber. Easy-to-follow guide offers advice on how to attract the greatest diversity of birds: birdhouses, feeders, water and waterers, much more. 96pp. 5³⁄₁₆ x 8¼. 28927-3

MEDICINAL AND OTHER USES OF NORTH AMERICAN PLANTS: A Historical Survey with Special Reference to the Eastern Indian Tribes, Charlotte Erichsen-Brown. Chronological historical citations document 500 years of usage of plants, trees, shrubs native to eastern Canada, northeastern U.S. Also complete identifying information. 343 illustrations. 544pp. 6½ x 9¼. 25951-X

STORYBOOK MAZES, Dave Phillips. 23 stories and mazes on two-page spreads: Wizard of Oz, Treasure Island, Robin Hood, etc. Solutions. 64pp. 8¼ x 11. 23628-5

AMERICAN NEGRO SONGS: 230 Folk Songs and Spirituals, Religious and Secular, John W. Work. This authoritative study traces the African influences of songs sung and played by black Americans at work, in church, and as entertainment. The author discusses the lyric significance of such songs as "Swing Low, Sweet Chariot," "John Henry," and others and offers the words and music for 230 songs. Bibliography. Index of Song Titles. 272pp. 6½ x 9¼. 40271-1

MOVIE-STAR PORTRAITS OF THE FORTIES, John Kobal (ed.). 163 glamor, studio photos of 106 stars of the 1940s: Rita Hayworth, Ava Gardner, Marlon Brando, Clark Gable, many more. 176pp. 8⅜ x 11¼. 23546-7

BENCHLEY LOST AND FOUND, Robert Benchley. Finest humor from early 30s, about pet peeves, child psychologists, post office and others. Mostly unavailable elsewhere. 73 illustrations by Peter Arno and others. 183pp. 5⅜ x 8½. 22410-4

YEKL and THE IMPORTED BRIDEGROOM AND OTHER STORIES OF YIDDISH NEW YORK, Abraham Cahan. Film Hester Street based on *Yekl* (1896). Novel, other stories among first about Jewish immigrants on N.Y.'s East Side. 240pp. 5⅜ x 8½. 22427-9

SELECTED POEMS, Walt Whitman. Generous sampling from *Leaves of Grass*. Twenty-four poems include "I Hear America Singing," "Song of the Open Road," "I Sing the Body Electric," "When Lilacs Last in the Dooryard Bloom'd," "O Captain! My Captain!"—all reprinted from an authoritative edition. Lists of titles and first lines. 128pp. 5³⁄₁₆ x 8¼. 26878-0

THE BEST TALES OF HOFFMANN, E. T. A. Hoffmann. 10 of Hoffmann's most important stories: "Nutcracker and the King of Mice," "The Golden Flowerpot," etc. 458pp. 5⅜ x 8½.   21793-0

FROM FETISH TO GOD IN ANCIENT EGYPT, E. A. Wallis Budge. Rich detailed survey of Egyptian conception of "God" and gods, magic, cult of animals, Osiris, more. Also, superb English translations of hymns and legends. 240 illustrations. 545pp. 5⅜ x 8½.   25803-3

FRENCH STORIES/CONTES FRANÇAIS: A Dual-Language Book, Wallace Fowlie. Ten stories by French masters, Voltaire to Camus: "Micromegas" by Voltaire; "The Atheist's Mass" by Balzac; "Minuet" by de Maupassant; "The Guest" by Camus, six more. Excellent English translations on facing pages. Also French-English vocabulary list, exercises, more. 352pp. 5⅜ x 8½.   26443-2

CHICAGO AT THE TURN OF THE CENTURY IN PHOTOGRAPHS: 122 Historic Views from the Collections of the Chicago Historical Society, Larry A. Viskochil. Rare large-format prints offer detailed views of City Hall, State Street, the Loop, Hull House, Union Station, many other landmarks, circa 1904-1913. Introduction. Captions. Maps. 144pp. 9⅜ x 12¼.   24656-6

OLD BROOKLYN IN EARLY PHOTOGRAPHS, 1865-1929, William Lee Younger. Luna Park, Gravesend race track, construction of Grand Army Plaza, moving of Hotel Brighton, etc. 157 previously unpublished photographs. 165pp. 8⅞ x 11¾.
23587-4

THE MYTHS OF THE NORTH AMERICAN INDIANS, Lewis Spence. Rich anthology of the myths and legends of the Algonquins, Iroquois, Pawnees and Sioux, prefaced by an extensive historical and ethnological commentary. 36 illustrations. 480pp. 5⅜ x 8½.   25967-6

AN ENCYCLOPEDIA OF BATTLES: Accounts of Over 1,560 Battles from 1479 B.C. to the Present, David Eggenberger. Essential details of every major battle in recorded history from the first battle of Megiddo in 1479 B.C. to Grenada in 1984. List of Battle Maps. New Appendix covering the years 1967-1984. Index. 99 illustrations. 544pp. 6½ x 9¼.   24913-1

SAILING ALONE AROUND THE WORLD, Captain Joshua Slocum. First man to sail around the world, alone, in small boat. One of great feats of seamanship told in delightful manner. 67 illustrations. 294pp. 5⅜ x 8½.   20326-3

ANARCHISM AND OTHER ESSAYS, Emma Goldman. Powerful, penetrating, prophetic essays on direct action, role of minorities, prison reform, puritan hypocrisy, violence, etc. 271pp. 5⅜ x 8½.   22484-8

MYTHS OF THE HINDUS AND BUDDHISTS, Ananda K. Coomaraswamy and Sister Nivedita. Great stories of the epics; deeds of Krishna, Shiva, taken from puranas, Vedas, folk tales; etc. 32 illustrations. 400pp. 5⅜ x 8½.   21759-0

THE TRAUMA OF BIRTH, Otto Rank. Rank's controversial thesis that anxiety neurosis is caused by profound psychological trauma which occurs at birth. 256pp. 5⅜ x 8½.   27974-X

A THEOLOGICO-POLITICAL TREATISE, Benedict Spinoza. Also contains unfinished Political Treatise. Great classic on religious liberty, theory of government on common consent. R. Elwes translation. Total of 421pp. 5⅜ x 8½.   20249-6

MY BONDAGE AND MY FREEDOM, Frederick Douglass. Born a slave, Douglass became outspoken force in antislavery movement. The best of Douglass' autobiographies. Graphic description of slave life. 464pp. 5⅜ x 8½. 22457-0

FOLLOWING THE EQUATOR: A Journey Around the World, Mark Twain. Fascinating humorous account of 1897 voyage to Hawaii, Australia, India, New Zealand, etc. Ironic, bemused reports on peoples, customs, climate, flora and fauna, politics, much more. 197 illustrations. 720pp. 5⅜ x 8½. 26113-1

THE PEOPLE CALLED SHAKERS, Edward D. Andrews. Definitive study of Shakers: origins, beliefs, practices, dances, social organization, furniture and crafts, etc. 33 illustrations. 351pp. 5⅜ x 8½. 21081-2

THE MYTHS OF GREECE AND ROME, H. A. Guerber. A classic of mythology, generously illustrated, long prized for its simple, graphic, accurate retelling of the principal myths of Greece and Rome, and for its commentary on their origins and significance. With 64 illustrations by Michelangelo, Raphael, Titian, Rubens, Canova, Bernini and others. 480pp. 5⅜ x 8½. 27584-1

PSYCHOLOGY OF MUSIC, Carl E. Seashore. Classic work discusses music as a medium from psychological viewpoint. Clear treatment of physical acoustics, auditory apparatus, sound perception, development of musical skills, nature of musical feeling, host of other topics. 88 figures. 408pp. 5⅜ x 8½. 21851-1

THE PHILOSOPHY OF HISTORY, Georg W. Hegel. Great classic of Western thought develops concept that history is not chance but rational process, the evolution of freedom. 457pp. 5⅜ x 8½. 20112-0

THE BOOK OF TEA, Kakuzo Okakura. Minor classic of the Orient: entertaining, charming explanation, interpretation of traditional Japanese culture in terms of tea ceremony. 94pp. 5⅜ x 8½. 20070-1

LIFE IN ANCIENT EGYPT, Adolf Erman. Fullest, most thorough, detailed older account with much not in more recent books, domestic life, religion, magic, medicine, commerce, much more. Many illustrations reproduce tomb paintings, carvings, hieroglyphs, etc. 597pp. 5⅜ x 8½. 22632-8

SUNDIALS, Their Theory and Construction, Albert Waugh. Far and away the best, most thorough coverage of ideas, mathematics concerned, types, construction, adjusting anywhere. Simple, nontechnical treatment allows even children to build several of these dials. Over 100 illustrations. 230pp. 5⅜ x 8½. 22947-5

THEORETICAL HYDRODYNAMICS, L. M. Milne-Thomson. Classic exposition of the mathematical theory of fluid motion, applicable to both hydrodynamics and aerodynamics. Over 600 exercises. 768pp. 6⅛ x 9¼. 68970-0

SONGS OF EXPERIENCE: Facsimile Reproduction with 26 Plates in Full Color, William Blake. 26 full-color plates from a rare 1826 edition. Includes "The Tyger," "London," "Holy Thursday," and other poems. Printed text of poems. 48pp. 5¼ x 7. 24636-1

OLD-TIME VIGNETTES IN FULL COLOR, Carol Belanger Grafton (ed.). Over 390 charming, often sentimental illustrations, selected from archives of Victorian graphics—pretty women posing, children playing, food, flowers, kittens and puppies, smiling cherubs, birds and butterflies, much more. All copyright-free. 48pp. 9¼ x 12¼. 27269-9

PERSPECTIVE FOR ARTISTS, Rex Vicat Cole. Depth, perspective of sky and sea, shadows, much more, not usually covered. 391 diagrams, 81 reproductions of drawings and paintings. 279pp. 5⅜ x 8½. 22487-2

DRAWING THE LIVING FIGURE, Joseph Sheppard. Innovative approach to artistic anatomy focuses on specifics of surface anatomy, rather than muscles and bones. Over 170 drawings of live models in front, back and side views, and in widely varying poses. Accompanying diagrams. 177 illustrations. Introduction. Index. 144pp. 8⅜ x11¼. 26723-7

GOTHIC AND OLD ENGLISH ALPHABETS: 100 Complete Fonts, Dan X. Solo. Add power, elegance to posters, signs, other graphics with 100 stunning copyright-free alphabets: Blackstone, Dolbey, Germania, 97 more—including many lower-case, numerals, punctuation marks. 104pp. 8⅛ x 11. 24695-7

HOW TO DO BEADWORK, Mary White. Fundamental book on craft from simple projects to five-bead chains and woven works. 106 illustrations. 142pp. 5⅜ x 8. 20697-1

THE BOOK OF WOOD CARVING, Charles Marshall Sayers. Finest book for beginners discusses fundamentals and offers 34 designs. "Absolutely first rate . . . well thought out and well executed."–E. J. Tangerman. 118pp. 7¾ x 10⅝. 23654-4

ILLUSTRATED CATALOG OF CIVIL WAR MILITARY GOODS: Union Army Weapons, Insignia, Uniform Accessories, and Other Equipment, Schuyler, Hartley, and Graham. Rare, profusely illustrated 1846 catalog includes Union Army uniform and dress regulations, arms and ammunition, coats, insignia, flags, swords, rifles, etc. 226 illustrations. 160pp. 9 x 12. 24939-5

WOMEN'S FASHIONS OF THE EARLY 1900s: An Unabridged Republication of "New York Fashions, 1909," National Cloak & Suit Co. Rare catalog of mail-order fashions documents women's and children's clothing styles shortly after the turn of the century. Captions offer full descriptions, prices. Invaluable resource for fashion, costume historians. Approximately 725 illustrations. 128pp. 8⅜ x 11¼. 27276-1

THE 1912 AND 1915 GUSTAV STICKLEY FURNITURE CATALOGS, Gustav Stickley. With over 200 detailed illustrations and descriptions, these two catalogs are essential reading and reference materials and identification guides for Stickley furniture. Captions cite materials, dimensions and prices. 112pp. 6½ x 9¼. 26676-1

EARLY AMERICAN LOCOMOTIVES, John H. White, Jr. Finest locomotive engravings from early 19th century: historical (1804–74), main-line (after 1870), special, foreign, etc. 147 plates. 142pp. 11⅜ x 8¼. 22772-3

THE TALL SHIPS OF TODAY IN PHOTOGRAPHS, Frank O. Braynard. Lavishly illustrated tribute to nearly 100 majestic contemporary sailing vessels: Amerigo Vespucci, Clearwater, Constitution, Eagle, Mayflower, Sea Cloud, Victory, many more. Authoritative captions provide statistics, background on each ship. 190 black-and-white photographs and illustrations. Introduction. 128pp. 8⅞ x 11¾. 27163-3

LITTLE BOOK OF EARLY AMERICAN CRAFTS AND TRADES, Peter Stockham (ed.). 1807 children's book explains crafts and trades: baker, hatter, cooper, potter, and many others. 23 copperplate illustrations. 140pp. 4⅝ x 6. 23336-7

VICTORIAN FASHIONS AND COSTUMES FROM HARPER'S BAZAR, 1867–1898, Stella Blum (ed.). Day costumes, evening wear, sports clothes, shoes, hats, other accessories in over 1,000 detailed engravings. 320pp. 9⅜ x 12¼. 22990-4

GUSTAV STICKLEY, THE CRAFTSMAN, Mary Ann Smith. Superb study surveys broad scope of Stickley's achievement, especially in architecture. Design philosophy, rise and fall of the Craftsman empire, descriptions and floor plans for many Craftsman houses, more. 86 black-and-white halftones. 31 line illustrations. Introduction 208pp. 6½ x 9¼. 27210-9

THE LONG ISLAND RAIL ROAD IN EARLY PHOTOGRAPHS, Ron Ziel. Over 220 rare photos, informative text document origin (1844) and development of rail service on Long Island. Vintage views of early trains, locomotives, stations, passengers, crews, much more. Captions. 8⅞ x 11¾. 26301-0

VOYAGE OF THE LIBERDADE, Joshua Slocum. Great 19th-century mariner's thrilling, first-hand account of the wreck of his ship off South America, the 35-foot boat he built from the wreckage, and its remarkable voyage home. 128pp. 5⅜ x 8½. 40022-0

TEN BOOKS ON ARCHITECTURE, Vitruvius. The most important book ever written on architecture. Early Roman aesthetics, technology, classical orders, site selection, all other aspects. Morgan translation. 331pp. 5⅜ x 8½. 20645-9

THE HUMAN FIGURE IN MOTION, Eadweard Muybridge. More than 4,500 stopped-action photos, in action series, showing undraped men, women, children jumping, lying down, throwing, sitting, wrestling, carrying, etc. 390pp. 7⅞ x 10⅝. 20204-6 Clothbd.

TREES OF THE EASTERN AND CENTRAL UNITED STATES AND CANADA, William M. Harlow. Best one-volume guide to 140 trees. Full descriptions, woodlore, range, etc. Over 600 illustrations. Handy size. 288pp. 4½ x 6⅜. 20395-6

SONGS OF WESTERN BIRDS, Dr. Donald J. Borror. Complete song and call repertoire of 60 western species, including flycatchers, juncoes, cactus wrens, many more–includes fully illustrated booklet. Cassette and manual 99913-0

GROWING AND USING HERBS AND SPICES, Milo Miloradovich. Versatile handbook provides all the information needed for cultivation and use of all the herbs and spices available in North America. 4 illustrations. Index. Glossary. 236pp. 5⅜ x 8½. 25058-X

BIG BOOK OF MAZES AND LABYRINTHS, Walter Shepherd. 50 mazes and labyrinths in all–classical, solid, ripple, and more–in one great volume. Perfect inexpensive puzzler for clever youngsters. Full solutions. 112pp. 8⅛ x 11. 22951-3

PIANO TUNING, J. Cree Fischer. Clearest, best book for beginner, amateur. Simple repairs, raising dropped notes, tuning by easy method of flattened fifths. No previous skills needed. 4 illustrations. 201pp. 5⅜ x 8½.   23267-0

HINTS TO SINGERS, Lillian Nordica. Selecting the right teacher, developing confidence, overcoming stage fright, and many other important skills receive thoughtful discussion in this indispensible guide, written by a world-famous diva of four decades' experience. 96pp. 5⅜ x 8½.   40094-8

THE COMPLETE NONSENSE OF EDWARD LEAR, Edward Lear. All nonsense limericks, zany alphabets, Owl and Pussycat, songs, nonsense botany, etc., illustrated by Lear. Total of 320pp. 5⅜ x 8½. (Available in U.S. only.)   20167-8

VICTORIAN PARLOUR POETRY: An Annotated Anthology, Michael R. Turner. 117 gems by Longfellow, Tennyson, Browning, many lesser-known poets. "The Village Blacksmith," "Curfew Must Not Ring Tonight," "Only a Baby Small," dozens more, often difficult to find elsewhere. Index of poets, titles, first lines. xxiii + 325pp. 5⅜ x 8¼.   27044-0

DUBLINERS, James Joyce. Fifteen stories offer vivid, tightly focused observations of the lives of Dublin's poorer classes. At least one, "The Dead," is considered a masterpiece. Reprinted complete and unabridged from standard edition. 160pp. 5³⁄₁₆ x 8¼.   26870-5

GREAT WEIRD TALES: 14 Stories by Lovecraft, Blackwood, Machen and Others, S. T. Joshi (ed.). 14 spellbinding tales, including "The Sin Eater," by Fiona McLeod, "The Eye Above the Mantel," by Frank Belknap Long, as well as renowned works by R. H. Barlow, Lord Dunsany, Arthur Machen, W. C. Morrow and eight other masters of the genre. 256pp. 5⅜ x 8½. (Available in U.S. only.)   40436-6

THE BOOK OF THE SACRED MAGIC OF ABRAMELIN THE MAGE, translated by S. MacGregor Mathers. Medieval manuscript of ceremonial magic. Basic document in Aleister Crowley, Golden Dawn groups. 268pp. 5⅜ x 8½.   23211-5

NEW RUSSIAN-ENGLISH AND ENGLISH-RUSSIAN DICTIONARY, M. A. O'Brien. This is a remarkably handy Russian dictionary, containing a surprising amount of information, including over 70,000 entries. 366pp. 4½ x 6⅛.   20208-9

HISTORIC HOMES OF THE AMERICAN PRESIDENTS, Second, Revised Edition, Irvin Haas. A traveler's guide to American Presidential homes, most open to the public, depicting and describing homes occupied by every American President from George Washington to George Bush. With visiting hours, admission charges, travel routes. 175 photographs. Index. 160pp. 8¼ x 11.   26751-2

NEW YORK IN THE FORTIES, Andreas Feininger. 162 brilliant photographs by the well-known photographer, formerly with *Life* magazine. Commuters, shoppers, Times Square at night, much else from city at its peak. Captions by John von Hartz. 181pp. 9¼ x 10¾.   23585-8

INDIAN SIGN LANGUAGE, William Tomkins. Over 525 signs developed by Sioux and other tribes. Written instructions and diagrams. Also 290 pictographs. 111pp. 6⅛ x 9¼.   22029-X

ANATOMY: A Complete Guide for Artists, Joseph Sheppard. A master of figure drawing shows artists how to render human anatomy convincingly. Over 460 illustrations. 224pp. 8⅜ x 11¼. 27279-6

MEDIEVAL CALLIGRAPHY: Its History and Technique, Marc Drogin. Spirited history, comprehensive instruction manual covers 13 styles (ca. 4th century through 15th). Excellent photographs; directions for duplicating medieval techniques with modern tools. 224pp. 8⅜ x 11¼. 26142-5

DRIED FLOWERS: How to Prepare Them, Sarah Whitlock and Martha Rankin. Complete instructions on how to use silica gel, meal and borax, perlite aggregate, sand and borax, glycerine and water to create attractive permanent flower arrangements. 12 illustrations. 32pp. 5⅜ x 8½. 21802-3

EASY-TO-MAKE BIRD FEEDERS FOR WOODWORKERS, Scott D. Campbell. Detailed, simple-to-use guide for designing, constructing, caring for and using feeders. Text, illustrations for 12 classic and contemporary designs. 96pp. 5⅜ x 8½. 25847-5

SCOTTISH WONDER TALES FROM MYTH AND LEGEND, Donald A. Mackenzie. 16 lively tales tell of giants rumbling down mountainsides, of a magic wand that turns stone pillars into warriors, of gods and goddesses, evil hags, powerful forces and more. 240pp. 5⅜ x 8½. 29677-6

THE HISTORY OF UNDERCLOTHES, C. Willett Cunnington and Phyllis Cunnington. Fascinating, well-documented survey covering six centuries of English undergarments, enhanced with over 100 illustrations: 12th-century laced-up bodice, footed long drawers (1795), 19th-century bustles, 19th-century corsets for men, Victorian "bust improvers," much more. 272pp. 5⅜ x 8¼. 27124-2

ARTS AND CRAFTS FURNITURE: The Complete Brooks Catalog of 1912, Brooks Manufacturing Co. Photos and detailed descriptions of more than 150 now very collectible furniture designs from the Arts and Crafts movement depict davenports, settees, buffets, desks, tables, chairs, bedsteads, dressers and more, all built of solid, quarter-sawed oak. Invaluable for students and enthusiasts of antiques, Americana and the decorative arts. 80pp. 6½ x 9¼. 27471-3

WILBUR AND ORVILLE: A Biography of the Wright Brothers, Fred Howard. Definitive, crisply written study tells the full story of the brothers' lives and work. A vividly written biography, unparalleled in scope and color, that also captures the spirit of an extraordinary era. 560pp. 6⅛ x 9¼. 40297-5

THE ARTS OF THE SAILOR: Knotting, Splicing and Ropework, Hervey Garrett Smith. Indispensable shipboard reference covers tools, basic knots and useful hitches; handsewing and canvas work, more. Over 100 illustrations. Delightful reading for sea lovers. 256pp. 5⅜ x 8½. 26440-8

FRANK LLOYD WRIGHT'S FALLINGWATER: The House and Its History, Second, Revised Edition, Donald Hoffmann. A total revision–both in text and illustrations–of the standard document on Fallingwater, the boldest, most personal architectural statement of Wright's mature years, updated with valuable new material from the recently opened Frank Lloyd Wright Archives. "Fascinating"–*The New York Times*. 116 illustrations. 128pp. 9¼ x 10¾. 27430-6

CATALOG OF DOVER BOOKS

PHOTOGRAPHIC SKETCHBOOK OF THE CIVIL WAR, Alexander Gardner. 100 photos taken on field during the Civil War. Famous shots of Manassas Harper's Ferry, Lincoln, Richmond, slave pens, etc. 244pp. 10⅝ x 8¼. 22731-6

FIVE ACRES AND INDEPENDENCE, Maurice G. Kains. Great back-to-the-land classic explains basics of self-sufficient farming. The one book to get. 95 illustrations. 397pp. 5⅜ x 8½. 20974-1

SONGS OF EASTERN BIRDS, Dr. Donald J. Borror. Songs and calls of 60 species most common to eastern U.S.: warblers, woodpeckers, flycatchers, thrushes, larks, many more in high-quality recording. Cassette and manual 99912-2

A MODERN HERBAL, Margaret Grieve. Much the fullest, most exact, most useful compilation of herbal material. Gigantic alphabetical encyclopedia, from aconite to zedoary, gives botanical information, medical properties, folklore, economic uses, much else. Indispensable to serious reader. 161 illustrations. 888pp. 6½ x 9¼. 2-vol. set. (Available in U.S. only.) Vol. I: 22798-7
Vol. II: 22799-5

HIDDEN TREASURE MAZE BOOK, Dave Phillips. Solve 34 challenging mazes accompanied by heroic tales of adventure. Evil dragons, people-eating plants, blood-thirsty giants, many more dangerous adversaries lurk at every twist and turn. 34 mazes, stories, solutions. 48pp. 8¼ x 11. 24566-7

LETTERS OF W. A. MOZART, Wolfgang A. Mozart. Remarkable letters show bawdy wit, humor, imagination, musical insights, contemporary musical world; includes some letters from Leopold Mozart. 276pp. 5⅜ x 8½. 22859-2

BASIC PRINCIPLES OF CLASSICAL BALLET, Agrippina Vaganova. Great Russian theoretician, teacher explains methods for teaching classical ballet. 118 illustrations. 175pp. 5⅜ x 8½. 22036-2

THE JUMPING FROG, Mark Twain. Revenge edition. The original story of The Celebrated Jumping Frog of Calaveras County, a hapless French translation, and Twain's hilarious "retranslation" from the French. 12 illustrations. 66pp. 5⅜ x 8½. 22686-7

BEST REMEMBERED POEMS, Martin Gardner (ed.). The 126 poems in this superb collection of 19th- and 20th-century British and American verse range from Shelley's "To a Skylark" to the impassioned "Renascence" of Edna St. Vincent Millay and to Edward Lear's whimsical "The Owl and the Pussycat." 224pp. 5⅜ x 8½. 27165-X

COMPLETE SONNETS, William Shakespeare. Over 150 exquisite poems deal with love, friendship, the tyranny of time, beauty's evanescence, death and other themes in language of remarkable power, precision and beauty. Glossary of archaic terms. 80pp. 5³⁄₁₆ x 8¼. 26686-9

THE BATTLES THAT CHANGED HISTORY, Fletcher Pratt. Eminent historian profiles 16 crucial conflicts, ancient to modern, that changed the course of civilization. 352pp. 5⅜ x 8½. 41129-X

THE WIT AND HUMOR OF OSCAR WILDE, Alvin Redman (ed.). More than 1,000 ripostes, paradoxes, wisecracks: Work is the curse of the drinking classes; I can resist everything except temptation; etc. 258pp. 5⅜ x 8½. 20602-5

SHAKESPEARE LEXICON AND QUOTATION DICTIONARY, Alexander Schmidt. Full definitions, locations, shades of meaning in every word in plays and poems. More than 50,000 exact quotations. 1,485pp. 6½ x 9¼. 2-vol. set.
Vol. 1: 22726-X
Vol. 2: 22727-8

SELECTED POEMS, Emily Dickinson. Over 100 best-known, best-loved poems by one of America's foremost poets, reprinted from authoritative early editions. No comparable edition at this price. Index of first lines. 64pp. 5³⁄₁₆ x 8¼. 26466-1

THE INSIDIOUS DR. FU-MANCHU, Sax Rohmer. The first of the popular mystery series introduces a pair of English detectives to their archnemesis, the diabolical Dr. Fu-Manchu. Flavorful atmosphere, fast-paced action, and colorful characters enliven this classic of the genre. 208pp. 5³⁄₁₆ x 8¼. 29898-1

THE MALLEUS MALEFICARUM OF KRAMER AND SPRENGER, translated by Montague Summers. Full text of most important witchhunter's "bible," used by both Catholics and Protestants. 278pp. 6⅝ x 10. 22802-9

SPANISH STORIES/CUENTOS ESPAÑOLES: A Dual-Language Book, Angel Flores (ed.). Unique format offers 13 great stories in Spanish by Cervantes, Borges, others. Faithful English translations on facing pages. 352pp. 5⅜ x 8½. 25399-6

GARDEN CITY, LONG ISLAND, IN EARLY PHOTOGRAPHS, 1869–1919, Mildred H. Smith. Handsome treasury of 118 vintage pictures, accompanied by carefully researched captions, document the Garden City Hotel fire (1899), the Vanderbilt Cup Race (1908), the first airmail flight departing from the Nassau Boulevard Aerodrome (1911), and much more. 96pp. 8⅞ x 11¾. 40669-5

OLD QUEENS, N.Y., IN EARLY PHOTOGRAPHS, Vincent F. Seyfried and William Asadorian. Over 160 rare photographs of Maspeth, Jamaica, Jackson Heights, and other areas. Vintage views of DeWitt Clinton mansion, 1939 World's Fair and more. Captions. 192pp. 8⅞ x 11. 26358-4

CAPTURED BY THE INDIANS: 15 Firsthand Accounts, 1750-1870, Frederick Drimmer. Astounding true historical accounts of grisly torture, bloody conflicts, relentless pursuits, miraculous escapes and more, by people who lived to tell the tale. 384pp. 5⅜ x 8½. 24901-8

THE WORLD'S GREAT SPEECHES (Fourth Enlarged Edition), Lewis Copeland, Lawrence W. Lamm, and Stephen J. McKenna. Nearly 300 speeches provide public speakers with a wealth of updated quotes and inspiration–from Pericles' funeral oration and William Jennings Bryan's "Cross of Gold Speech" to Malcolm X's powerful words on the Black Revolution and Earl of Spenser's tribute to his sister, Diana, Princess of Wales. 944pp. 5⅜ x 8⅜. 40903-1

THE BOOK OF THE SWORD, Sir Richard F. Burton. Great Victorian scholar/adventurer's eloquent, erudite history of the "queen of weapons"–from prehistory to early Roman Empire. Evolution and development of early swords, variations (sabre, broadsword, cutlass, scimitar, etc.), much more. 336pp. 6⅛ x 9¼. 25434-8

AUTOBIOGRAPHY: The Story of My Experiments with Truth, Mohandas K. Gandhi. Boyhood, legal studies, purification, the growth of the Satyagraha (nonviolent protest) movement. Critical, inspiring work of the man responsible for the freedom of India. 480pp. 5⅜ x 8½. (Available in U.S. only.) 24593-4

CELTIC MYTHS AND LEGENDS, T. W. Rolleston. Masterful retelling of Irish and Welsh stories and tales. Cuchulain, King Arthur, Deirdre, the Grail, many more. First paperback edition. 58 full-page illustrations. 512pp. 5⅜ x 8½. 26507-2

THE PRINCIPLES OF PSYCHOLOGY, William James. Famous long course complete, unabridged. Stream of thought, time perception, memory, experimental methods; great work decades ahead of its time. 94 figures. 1,391pp. 5⅜ x 8½. 2-vol. set. Vol. I: 20381-6 Vol. II: 20382-4

THE WORLD AS WILL AND REPRESENTATION, Arthur Schopenhauer. Definitive English translation of Schopenhauer's life work, correcting more than 1,000 errors, omissions in earlier translations. Translated by E. F. J. Payne. Total of 1,269pp. 5⅜ x 8½. 2-vol. set. Vol. 1: 21761-2 Vol. 2: 21762-0

MAGIC AND MYSTERY IN TIBET, Madame Alexandra David-Neel. Experiences among lamas, magicians, sages, sorcerers, Bonpa wizards. A true psychic discovery. 32 illustrations. 321pp. 5⅜ x 8½. (Available in U.S. only.) 22682-4

THE EGYPTIAN BOOK OF THE DEAD, E. A. Wallis Budge. Complete reproduction of Ani's papyrus, finest ever found. Full hieroglyphic text, interlinear transliteration, word-for-word translation, smooth translation. 533pp. 6½ x 9¼. 21866-X

MATHEMATICS FOR THE NONMATHEMATICIAN, Morris Kline. Detailed, college-level treatment of mathematics in cultural and historical context, with numerous exercises. Recommended Reading Lists. Tables. Numerous figures. 641pp. 5⅜ x 8½. 24823-2

PROBABILISTIC METHODS IN THE THEORY OF STRUCTURES, Isaac Elishakoff. Well-written introduction covers the elements of the theory of probability from two or more random variables, the reliability of such multivariable structures, the theory of random function, Monte Carlo methods of treating problems incapable of exact solution, and more. Examples. 502pp. 5⅜ x 8½. 40691-1

THE RIME OF THE ANCIENT MARINER, Gustave Doré, S. T. Coleridge. Doré's finest work; 34 plates capture moods, subtleties of poem. Flawless full-size reproductions printed on facing pages with authoritative text of poem. "Beautiful. Simply beautiful."–*Publisher's Weekly.* 77pp. 9¼ x 12. 22305-1

NORTH AMERICAN INDIAN DESIGNS FOR ARTISTS AND CRAFTSPEOPLE, Eva Wilson. Over 360 authentic copyright-free designs adapted from Navajo blankets, Hopi pottery, Sioux buffalo hides, more. Geometrics, symbolic figures, plant and animal motifs, etc. 128pp. 8⅜ x 11. (Not for sale in the United Kingdom.) 25341-4

SCULPTURE: Principles and Practice, Louis Slobodkin. Step-by-step approach to clay, plaster, metals, stone; classical and modern. 253 drawings, photos. 255pp. 8⅛ x 11. 22960-2

THE INFLUENCE OF SEA POWER UPON HISTORY, 1660–1783, A. T. Mahan. Influential classic of naval history and tactics still used as text in war colleges. First paperback edition. 4 maps. 24 battle plans. 640pp. 5⅜ x 8½. 25509-3

CATALOG OF DOVER BOOKS

THE STORY OF THE TITANIC AS TOLD BY ITS SURVIVORS, Jack Winocour (ed.). What it was really like. Panic, despair, shocking inefficiency, and a little heroism. More thrilling than any fictional account. 26 illustrations. 320pp. $5\frac{3}{8}$ x $8\frac{1}{2}$. 20610-6

FAIRY AND FOLK TALES OF THE IRISH PEASANTRY, William Butler Yeats (ed.). Treasury of 64 tales from the twilight world of Celtic myth and legend: "The Soul Cages," "The Kildare Pooka," "King O'Toole and his Goose," many more. Introduction and Notes by W. B. Yeats. 352pp. $5\frac{3}{8}$ x $8\frac{1}{2}$. 26941-8

BUDDHIST MAHAYANA TEXTS, E. B. Cowell and others (eds.). Superb, accurate translations of basic documents in Mahayana Buddhism, highly important in history of religions. The Buddha-karita of Asvaghosha, Larger Sukhavativyuha, more. 448pp. $5\frac{3}{8}$ x $8\frac{1}{2}$. 25552-2

ONE TWO THREE . . . INFINITY: Facts and Speculations of Science, George Gamow. Great physicist's fascinating, readable overview of contemporary science: number theory, relativity, fourth dimension, entropy, genes, atomic structure, much more. 128 illustrations. Index. 352pp. $5\frac{3}{8}$ x $8\frac{1}{2}$. 25664-2

EXPERIMENTATION AND MEASUREMENT, W. J. Youden. Introductory manual explains laws of measurement in simple terms and offers tips for achieving accuracy and minimizing errors. Mathematics of measurement, use of instruments, experimenting with machines. 1994 edition. Foreword. Preface. Introduction. Epilogue. Selected Readings. Glossary. Index. Tables and figures. 128pp. $5\frac{3}{8}$ x $8\frac{1}{2}$. 40451-X

DALÍ ON MODERN ART: The Cuckolds of Antiquated Modern Art, Salvador Dalí. Influential painter skewers modern art and its practitioners. Outrageous evaluations of Picasso, Cézanne, Turner, more. 15 renderings of paintings discussed. 44 calligraphic decorations by Dalí. 96pp. $5\frac{3}{8}$ x $8\frac{1}{2}$. (Available in U.S. only.) 29220-7

ANTIQUE PLAYING CARDS: A Pictorial History, Henry René D'Allemagne. Over 900 elaborate, decorative images from rare playing cards (14th–20th centuries): Bacchus, death, dancing dogs, hunting scenes, royal coats of arms, players cheating, much more. 96pp. $9\frac{1}{4}$ x $12\frac{1}{4}$. 29265-7

MAKING FURNITURE MASTERPIECES: 30 Projects with Measured Drawings, Franklin H. Gottshall. Step-by-step instructions, illustrations for constructing handsome, useful pieces, among them a Sheraton desk, Chippendale chair, Spanish desk, Queen Anne table and a William and Mary dressing mirror. 224pp. $8\frac{1}{8}$ x $11\frac{1}{4}$. 29338-6

THE FOSSIL BOOK: A Record of Prehistoric Life, Patricia V. Rich et al. Profusely illustrated definitive guide covers everything from single-celled organisms and dinosaurs to birds and mammals and the interplay between climate and man. Over 1,500 illustrations. 760pp. $7\frac{1}{2}$ x $10\frac{1}{8}$. 29371-8

Paperbound unless otherwise indicated. Available at your book dealer, online at **www.doverpublications.com**, or by writing to Dept. GI, Dover Publications, Inc., 31 East 2nd Street, Mineola, NY 11501. For current price information or for free catalogues (please indicate field of interest), write to Dover Publications or log on to **www.doverpublications.com** and see every Dover book in print. Dover publishes more than 500 books each year on science, elementary and advanced mathematics, biology, music, art, literary history, social sciences, and other areas.